SCARY STORIES

FOR WHEN YOU'RE HOME ALONE

ALLEN B. URY

ILLUSTRATIONS BY ERIC REESE

Lowell House
Juvenile
Los Angeles

CONTEMPORARY BOOKS
Chicago

Cover illustration by Bernard Custodio

Library of Congress Catalog Card Number: 96-33909
ISBN: 1-56565-383-1

Publisher: Jack Artenstein
General Manager, Juvenile Division: Elizabeth D. Amos
Director of Publishing Services: Rena Copperman
Editor-in-Chief, Juvenile Fiction: Barbara Schoichet
Managing Editor, Juvenile Division: Lindsey Hay
Art Director: Lisa-Theresa Lenthall

Lowell House books can be purchased at special discounts when
ordered in bulk for premiums and special sales. Contact Department
JH at the following address:

Lowell House Juvenile
2029 Century Park East
Suite 3290
Los Angeles, CA 90067

Manufactured in the United States of America
10 9 8 7 6 5 4 3 2 1

Contents

For DesertMom
—A. B. U.

RONNIE'S ROCKET

Ronnie Ormsby had been riding his Chesterfield Bronco bicycle ever since the third grade. Low-slung with a long "banana" seat and high, U-shaped handle bars, the bike had been hopelessly out-of-date when his parents bought it for him on sale at a local discount store five years ago. Now it was an embarrassment.

"I need a new bike," Ronnie told his mother one day.

"Really? What's wrong with the one you have?" his mother asked skeptically.

"It's too small," Ronnie insisted. "It only has one speed. And it's old-fashioned. I mean, come on, Mom, I've had it for five years already."

"We've had *you* for thirteen years, and you don't see us trading *you* in," his mother replied with a grin.

"That's different!" Ronnie objected. "People grow up. Bikes just get old. And all the kids at school make fun of me. They say my bike is for dweebs."

"Are you a dweeb?" his mother asked calmly.

"No way!" Ronnie cried.

"Then I guess your friends are wrong," his mother concluded, giving her son a warm pat on the back.

Fuming with frustration, Ronnie turned away and was about to storm out of the kitchen when his mother picked up a flyer off the table.

"They're having a neighborhood garage sale over at Wilshire Estates this weekend," she said, referring to an upscale neighborhood about a half-mile from the apartment complex where the Ormsby family lived. "Why don't we check it out? Maybe we can find you a bike you'll like."

"Really?" Ronnie perked up.

"Assuming the price is right," his mother replied.

"Cool!" Ronnie exclaimed, then headed off to his room to imagine himself pedaling to school on a gleaming new 21-speed racing bike.

* * *

That Saturday, Ronnie and his mother drove over to Wilshire Estates while his dad stayed home to do some household repairs. For the next two hours they went from house to house sifting through other people's unwanted belongings looking for bargains, specifically a bike that would meet Ronnie's exacting standards.

For a while it looked like their quest was hopeless. Although Ronnie's mom found a used 35mm camera she liked and some classic '70s records she couldn't resist, Ronnie found his choice of bicycles to be painfully lean. Most of the bikes he saw were small, older models that were not much more stylish or attractive than the one he currently rode. Most, in fact, were ancient, rusty artifacts that looked like they'd been gathering dust in their owners' garages for the past millennium. Ronnie was all set to give up when he found a 26-inch Galaxy Rocket road bike for the incredibly low price of $50 for sale at the house at the end of Juniper Street.

The bicycle, one of the hottest designs around, was painted in an ultra-cool cobalt blue, had a soft, comfortable seat, and appeared to be in perfect mechanical condition. Ronnie knew that in stores a bike like this would sell for around $300. Getting one for $50 wasn't just a bargain, it was a *steal*!

"Mom, I just have to have this bike!" Ronnie insisted excitedly, dragging his mother over to the bicycle which sat among a large collection of boys' clothes and furniture. "You're never going to find a bike this good for a price this low. *Please!*"

His mother stood in thoughtful silence for a moment or two, then reached for her wallet. "All right," she said. "I just hope you're happy with it."

"Mom, believe me," Ronnie assured him. "This is a purchase you're never going to regret."

•   •   •

"Great bike!" remarked Leonard Bean as Ronnie pulled up to the bike rack in front of Robert E. Lee Junior High. "Is that yours?"

"All mine," Ronnie replied proudly as he jumped off his new bike and prepared to chain it into place. "I got it at a garage sale for fifty bucks."

"Fifty bucks? No way!" Leonard exclaimed. "That's a two-hundred dollar bike!"

"Three hundred," Ronnie corrected him. "But we got it used. The old owners just didn't want it anymore, I guess."

"Man, you are so lucky!" Leonard said, bending down to admire the bike's gleaming frame and padded handlebars. "Wow, the people you bought this from practically gave it away."

"I guess some of us just lead charmed lives," Ronnie said with a cocky grin as he and Leonard hurried into the school.

The day passed quickly for Ronnie, and at 3:30 that afternoon he was back on his new bicycle pedaling for home. The sky was clear and the air was warm, and Ronnie was feeling so good that he decided to take the long way back down Pine Avenue.

Coasting smoothly along past a block filled with small storefront merchants, Ronnie was approaching the stoplight at Prospect Street when his front wheel made a sudden jerk to the left. At first, he thought that he'd hit a pothole or some other obstruction, and quickly recovered his balance. But seconds later, the bike jerked again, and this time Ronnie couldn't straighten it out, no matter how hard he tried.

Terrified, he found himself careening into the middle of the busy street. Horns honked angrily and brakes squealed in protest as cars and buses traveling in both directions stopped short to avoid colliding with the runaway bicycle.

Certain he was about to crash, Ronnie squeezed his hand brakes as hard as he could. But the bike failed to

stop, or even slow down. As angry drivers yelled at him to watch where he was going, Ronnie spun around until the bike and the boy were facing back in the direction from which they'd come. Then the Rocket began to accelerate, picking up speed even though Ronnie was holding the peddles firmly in place.

"Help!" Ronnie screamed in terror as the Rocket continued to race down Pine Avenue like a runaway motorcycle. "I can't stop!"

Desperate to regain control of his bike, Ronnie straightened his legs in an attempt to brake himself against the pavement. But being only five feet tall, his shoes didn't even come close to touching the street.

Next he tried steering himself into the curb, but no matter how much force he exerted against the handlebars, the bike refused to budge from its course. It was as if the Rocket had a mind of its own.

After speeding straight through a stop sign, the wayward bike now carried Ronnie up one more block, then turned right onto Loyola Boulevard. At this point, it positioned itself directly behind a large, black, American made sedan which had made the same turn just a few moments before.

At the next block, the sedan slowed down and paused briefly at a stop sign. Amazingly, the Rocket slowed as well, finally coming to a complete stop. Ronnie heaved a sigh of relief.

It's finally over! he thought thankfully. *I hope that never happens again!*

However, as soon as the black sedan resumed its course, his bike leaped back into motion, carrying Ronnie with it. Slowly, it began to dawn on Ronnie that his bicycle was following this specific car. For reasons Ronnie could not explain, and powered by forces he could never imagine, the Rocket appeared determined to tail this automobile wherever it went. But for what purpose, Ronnie wondered, holding on for his life. And how long was he expected to remain aboard?

Fifteen minutes later, the mysterious black sedan was accelerating onto Interstate 14, a four-lane highway where cars, trucks, and other motorized vehicles regularly traveled at sixty miles per hour and sometimes even faster. Totally terrified, Ronnie realized that if his bike continued to follow the automobile, he would soon be traveling at speeds far too dangerous for any mere thirteen-year-old to attempt. He had no choice but to jump off the bike while he still could.

Steeling himself as the crazed bike approached the highway's on-ramp, Ronnie threw his right leg over the center bar, then launched himself toward a landscaped area that was bordering the roadway. He landed with a painful *thump*, and rolled several times before finally coming to a halt. At the same time, the Rocket lost all stability and came crashing to a stop on the pavement beside him.

Gasping breathlessly, Ronnie slowly got to his feet, brushed himself off, and went to inspect his seemingly possessed bicycle. As far as he could see, the crash had not caused any serious damage to the machine. Almost afraid to touch the Rocket for fear that it would again jump to life, Ronnie gently grabbed hold of the metal frame and carefully set the bicycle upright. Then, he oh-so-cautiously sat himself on the seat and pulled the handlebars back and forth. The front wheel moved freely.

There was no resistance from the bike, no attempt to go speeding off after the black sedan. Apparently, whatever magical force had taken control of the Rocket, had left as quickly as it had come. As for Ronnie, he hoped it would never return . . . and that by the time he got home he'd come up with a good explanation for why he was coming home from school so late.

●   ●   ●

"Wow, that is so weird," Leonard gasped the next morning after Ronnie told him the story about the runaway Rocket. "At least now you know why the original owners let it go so cheap."

"What do you mean?" Ronnie asked, unsure of what his friend was suggesting.

"Obviously, the bike is haunted," Leonard explained. "It probably contains the ghost of its original owner. Or maybe it's haunted by some guy who got killed when it was made at the bicycle factory."

"That's ridiculous," Ronnie scoffed. "There's no such thing as ghosts—or haunted bicycles!"

"So how do *you* explain it?" Leonard demanded. "Bikes don't usually go around chasing after cars all on their own."

Ronnie had to admit that his friend had a point. Chances are, his bike was haunted. That left him with only two choices. Either he could sell the bike to someone else, or he could try to find a way to rid the machine of its spectral guest. Since he loved the Rocket more than anything he'd ever owned, and since the chances of getting another one like it for $50 were slim to none, he decided that getting rid of the spirit was his only option. But how? He decided to start at the beginning—the house at the end of Juniper Street.

* * *

"Yes? Can I help you?" the middle-aged woman standing at the front door asked. Ronnie remembered her as being the person who had sold his mother the Rocket that previous weekend. He remembered her short brown hair and high-tech athletic shoes. But most of all, he remembered her sad, woeful eyes.

"My name's Ronnie Ormsby," Ronnie said. "I don't know if you remember me, but my mom bought that bike from you last weekend."

The woman looked over at the cobalt-blue Rocket on the nearby sidewalk. Immediately, Ronnie could see her facial muscles tighten and heard a breath suddenly catch in her throat.

"Is there something wrong?" the woman asked, quickly regaining control of herself. "Don't you like it?"

"It's great," Ronnie said, having long ago decided that accusing the woman of selling him a haunted bicycle was probably not the best way to begin their conversation. "I was just wondering if you could tell me who it belonged to originally."

The woman hesitated a moment, then cast her sad eyes downward.

"It belonged to my son, David," she replied, her voice shaky. "He died last year."

"I'm sorry," Ronnie said, suddenly feeling very awkward. Still, he knew he had to get to the bottom of this mystery, so he pressed ahead. "I don't mean to be nosy, but can you tell me *how* he died?"

Again, the woman paused before responding, her eyes going blank as her thoughts drifted into the past. "He was run off the road," she finally replied. "He was riding his bike—*that* bike—along Canyon Road when someone forced him off the edge. He fell into the canyon and was killed on impact. Somehow the bike itself was barely scratched. At first, my husband and I couldn't bear to part with anything that belonged to him. But finally we decided it was time to move on. That's why we had the garage sale—to sell off David's things."

Ronnie thought back to the previous weekend. He remembered the bed, furniture, and other items this family had set out for sale. It must have been just about everything from David's bedroom. Ronnie could only imagine how much it must have hurt this woman and her husband to see it all go.

"Why did you want to know about David?" the woman inquired.

"I, uh, was just curious," Ronnie replied with a shrug. Then he added, "By the way, did they ever find out who forced David off the road?"

"No, they didn't," the woman said, her voice tinged with anger. "The police believe it was a drunk driver. He probably never even saw David or knew what he did."

Ronnie thanked the woman for her time, hopped back on his Rocket, and pedaled for home. He now believed he understood exactly what was going on. Just like some spirits haunt the houses in which they died, David's ghost was living inside the bicycle on which he was killed. But he wasn't just hanging around for the fun of it. He had a mission to find the person who had killed him and, if possible, bring him to justice. Ronnie realized that, like it or not, he had been recruited to help in this mission, and that the Rocket would not truly be his until David's soul could rest in peace.

* * *

The next week, for two hours each day after school, Ronnie rode his Rocket up and down Pine Avenue hoping to encounter once again the black sedan the bike had been so interested in. But as days past without even the slightest sign of life from the machine, Ronnie began to think that either the car would never show up, or David's ghost had already abandoned the bike and had moved on to, well, wherever spirits ultimately go.

And then, on his tenth attempt to locate the killer sedan, Ronnie's luck changed. He was cruising up Pine Avenue past Tubbman's Hardware Store when he felt the Rocket inexplicably pick up speed. At first Ronnie thought that he'd just been pushed forward by a gust of wind, but this notion was quickly dispelled when he applied the hand brakes and saw they had no effect.

It's happening again! Ronnie thought, his mind filled with a combination of giddy excitement and rising fear. *The bike is—alive!*

Holding tight, he crouched low over the handlebars as the bicycle continued to pick up speed. Once more moving with a mind of its own, it shot through the next intersection without even a pause, zig-zagged its way past several slower-moving cars, then whipped around onto Wilmington Avenue.

Immediately, Ronnie saw the black sedan dead ahead. The first thing he did was to pay attention to its license plate, knowing this would be the best way to ultimately identify its owner. He'd even brought a pencil and pad of paper with him to write down the number. But he was now traveling so fast—nearly thirty miles per hour—that he didn't dare release the handlebars to fish the items from his pocket.

"TGG0901," he said aloud as the license plate came clearly into view. He repeated the number over and over again, hoping to commit it to memory.

After several blocks, the sedan stopped, then turned onto Canyon Road, with the Rocket right behind it. Soon, both vehicles were speeding along the narrow, twisting asphalt ribbon, on one side of them a wall of high pine trees, on the other a narrow shoulder that dropped away into sheer oblivion.

This is where it happened! Ronnie thought in terror as he glanced over at the cliff below him. *This is where David was killed!*

As if confirming Ronnie's suspicions, the Rocket began to vibrate angrily and its speed increased even further. Ronnie hung on for dear life as he sped directly toward the back of the black sedan. He clenched his teeth and shut his eyes as—*thump!*—his front wheel slammed straight into the sedan's rear bumper. The bike slowed for a moment, then sped up again, striking the car ahead a second time.

"Stop it!" Ronnie screamed. "You're going to get me killed, too!"

Apparently, the sedan's driver had finally noticed Ronnie, for the car drifted toward the center of the road, giving him a little more room on the right. But instead of taking this route, which would have put the frightened boy between the car and the cliff, the bike jogged to the *left*, speeding up until Ronnie found himself even with the driver's window.

His heart racing even faster than the bike itself, Ronnie glanced to his right to see if he could identify the driver—the person who had been responsible for David's tragic death. But what he saw made his blood run cold. *There was no one there!*

Before he had a chance to react to this impossible sight, the Rocket veered to the right, slamming itself into the side of the sedan. The sedan, also acting on its own, veered left, forcing Ronnie toward the center line.

"Stop it!" Ronnie screamed again, uncertain if he was now talking to David's ghost or the ghostly car with which he was now locked in deadly combat. "I want to go home!"

Ignoring its young rider's pleas, the Rocket again slammed itself into the side of the driverless car. This time, the sedan drifted slightly toward the shoulder, then roared back toward Ronnie, determined to kill him.

At that very instant, the bike's brakes slammed into place. Sweating bullets, Ronnie clung desperately to the handlebars as he skidded wildly across the pavement. At the same time, the sedan shot straight in front of him, missing his front tire by mere inches, and continued to slide into the oncoming lane. A moment later, he heard the sound of a blaring truck horn and— *WHAM!*—the sedan collided head-on with a huge semi that had just emerged from around a blind curve.

There was a sickening explosion of glass and metal as the impact shattered the driverless sedan and sent its remnants flying directly over Ronnie's head, only to disappear into the canyon behind him.

It took nearly ten full seconds for the truck driver to bring his rig to a stop. Jumping from the cab, he ran over to the cliffside and peered into the chasm below. Ronnie joined him moments later, and together they gazed down at the burning remains of the murderous automobile.

"Crazy driver!" the trucker bellowed. "He plowed right into me! You saw it, didn't you, kid? You saw what he did!"

"I saw the whole thing," Ronnie said calmly.

"I better call the cops," the trucker said, running back to his nearby rig where he immediately got on his CB radio.

As the trucker continued to call in his emergency report, Ronnie climbed back onto his Rocket. He checked his brakes, his steering, and his gears. Everything seemed to be working just fine. Then, smiling with the knowledge that he had rid the world of an evil ghost driver that had killed who-knew-how-many defenseless kids, Ronnie turned around and pedaled toward home.

As he did, his bell rang twice . . . then fell silent.

Ronnie rang the bell back. "So long, David," he murmured. "Rest in peace."

THE PROMISE

A frigid wind blew through the open window. Twelve-year-old Natalie Archer shivered as she struggled to close it. "Brr!" she said, going back to sit next to her best friend, Megan Mitchell, who was lying on Natalie's bed, a social studies book opened before her.

"They say this winter's going to be really bad," Megan noted. "It's supposedly due to global warming."

"That's what I heard, too," Natalie agreed. "It's funny, but you'd think that if the world was getting warmer, the winters would be getting better, not worse."

"They say higher temperatures exaggerate everything, creating more hurricanes, tornadoes, and blizzards," Megan replied. "Some parts of the world are actually flooding, while others are starting to become deserts."

"Kind of makes you wonder what the world is going to be like when we grow up, doesn't it?" Natalie said with a sigh. "Or even if there's going to *be* a world."

"Oh, there's going to be a world," Megan assured her. "But who knows if we'll want to live in it."

"Wouldn't it be nice to have a time machine so you could go into the future to see what things will be like?" Natalie wondered aloud, her green eyes sparkling.

"Yeah, only there's just one problem," Megan noted. "What if you don't like what you see? I mean, if you knew something awful was going to happen, you might not even want to go on living."

"But if I could see the future, maybe I could change it," Natalie stated. "Maybe I could warn people and we could do things *now* to stop the disaster."

"Well, that's one problem we'll never have to worry about," Megan assured her. "I don't think they'll ever invent time travel. At least not in *our* lifetimes. What we have to worry about right now is our social studies test."

But Natalie wasn't ready to return to studying. The idea of time travel was one she'd always found particularly exciting. As a long-time science fiction fan, she had read about as many time travel stories as anyone her age could. She knew just about everything there was to know about "time paradoxes" and "alternate timelines," but until this very moment, she'd never really considered time travel in her lifetime. And then an idea struck her.

"Megan, I've decided to find out if time travel will ever be invented," Natalie declared. "At least, I'm going to find out if I'll ever be able to do it myself."

"How?" Megan asked skeptically.

"Easy," Natalie replied. "I'm going to promise myself right now that if I ever get hold of a time machine at any time in the future, I'll come back to when I was a kid and tell myself about it."

"You mean, if you get to use a time machine when you're say, fifty years old, you'll come back to right now?" Megan asked.

"Exactly," Natalie stated.

Just then, Natalie's bedroom door swung wide open. Startled, the girls turned, half-expecting to see a fifty-year-old Natalie Archer walking into the room. But instead of a time traveler, their visitor turned out to be Hairball, the Archer's orange and white tabby cat.

"Whoa, that was weird!" Natalie gasped, feeling her heart pounding in her chest. "I almost thought—"

"So did I!" Megan cried, giggling nervously. "I guess this means you won't ever get hold of a time machine."

Natalie frowned. "Why do you say that?"

"Because your future self isn't here right *now* like you promised," Megan explained. "Understand?"

Natalie still frowned, then her eyes lit up. "Okay, that might not have been a good test," she said. "After forty years, I probably forgot about this particular day and this particular minute. I've got to pick a special date I won't ever forget to return to."

"Like what?" asked Megan.

Natalie thought about this for a moment, then smiled. "My thirteenth birthday is coming up in March. I'm going to promise myself that if they ever invent a time machine, I'll come back to visit myself on my thirteenth birthday— that's a date I know I'll remember."

"What do you think your future self will look like?" Megan asked. "And how do you think you'll feel about seeing yourself as a grown-up?"

"Who knows?" Natalie replied with a shrug. "I suppose I'll feel, well, excited."

But the more Natalie thought about it, the more she wondered if seeing her own future would be exciting . . . or horrifying.

● ● ●

As usual, the first two months of winter flew by quickly. First there were preparations for Thanksgiving to keep everyone busy, followed by the whole Christmas season, and then New Year's Eve. But despite these distractions, Natalie Archer never forgot the promise she had made to herself, and she waited with painful anticipation for March to come. Somehow she was sure that her future self would not disappoint her.

As January turned to February, then February to March, the suspense grew and grew until Natalie was so excited she felt like she was going to burst.

"I can't wait, Megan!" she cried, barely able to sit still as she and her friend sat in the school cafeteria.

"Look, Natalie, you know that chances are *nothing's* going to happen tomorrow," Megan said, trying to lower Natalie's impossibly high expectations. It was already March 2nd, and Natalie had been so distracted all week that she could barely do her schoolwork. "You know, most scientists still think time travel is impossible."

"That's what they said about airplanes," Natalie shot back. "And space travel. And artificial intelligence."

"In one article I read, the author said that we know time travel will never be invented because if it ever was, travelers from the future would be with us right now," Megan pressed on. "Since no one has ever seen a time traveler, we know they'll never exist."

"That is so stupid!" Natalie protested. "What's a time traveler supposed to look like? As far we know, there are time travelers all over the place, only they dress like us and keep their mouths shut so they don't get locked up in some institution."

Megan sighed heavily. "I'm just afraid you're going to be disappointed," she said. "Just because you promise yourself something doesn't mean it's going to happen."

Down deep, Natalie knew her friend was right. Chances were, her thirteenth birthday would come and go just like any other birthday. Certainly there'd be nothing that would change the course of history—which is exactly what Natalie was hoping to do.

Still, there was that wild, visionary part of her that refused to give up, and later that night, as she lay in bed, she wondered what the following day would bring. If an older Natalie *did* appear, what kind of life would she tell her younger self she had to look forward to? Would there be world peace or endless wars? Would there be clean air or suffocating pollution? Would the future be bright or bleak?

It was midnight before Natalie finally fell asleep, and when she awoke the next morning, she half-expected to find her future self standing at the foot of the bed. But it didn't happen. Neither did the future Natalie show up at breakfast, at school, or on her way home.

By evening, Natalie had all but given up hope that the promise she'd made to herself was going to be kept. Although this harsh reality was disappointing, having to face it head-on was surprisingly easy to do.

"Hey, you win some, you lose some," she told Megan offhandedly that night during the birthday party her mother had arranged for her and six of her closest friends. "I mean, we all knew it was a longshot, right?"

"I'm glad to see you're taking it so well," Megan said. "For a while there, I thought if future Natalie didn't show up, you were going to go psychotic or something."

"Still, it would have been really cool," Natalie said, grabbing a pizza bagel from one of the trays her mom had set out in the family room.

Just then, the doorbell rang.

"That must be Wendy," Natalie said, heading for the front door. Wendy Neumann was one of the girls invited to help Natalie celebrate the big One-Three, and she was, as usual, a half hour late.

But when Natalie opened the door, it wasn't Wendy she found standing on the front stoop. It was a woman who appeared to be in her mid-forties. She stood about five-six, had short dark hair, and sparkling green eyes.

Natalie gasped when she saw the woman—and the woman herself also seemed taken aback. For a moment, each stood staring at the other in silent recognition . . . like long-lost sisters.

"Natalie Archer?" the woman asked.

"Uh-huh," Natalie replied, her mouth hanging open.

"I believe you're expecting me," the woman said.

"You mean—?" Natalie began, her question choking off in her throat.

The woman, equally unnerved, simply nodded.

"Who's there?" her mother asked, joining Natalie at the door.

"Mrs. Archer?" the visitor asked with a smile. "I'm Mrs. Gregorian, Natalie's science teacher. I just came by to talk to her about a school project."

Natalie grinned. Her science teacher's name *was* Mrs. Gregorian, and she knew that she and her mother had never met. *Very clever,* Natalie thought. *Even if I do say so myself.*

"Is there some problem?" Natalie's mom asked.

"No, no, no," the visitor assured her. "I just needed to ask Natalie some questions. May we talk for a moment?"

"Of course," Natalie's mom replied. "Come inside."

"No, that's all right. I wouldn't want to disturb the party," the visitor replied. "Really, I only need a moment of Natalie's time."

"All right," said Natalie's mom. Then she turned to her daughter. "Dinner will be ready in five minutes." And with that, she headed off to the kitchen.

Stepping outside and closing the door behind her, Natalie stood before the visitor . . . whom she now knew was, in fact, herself.

"I don't have much time, Natalie," the woman said urgently. "I'm part of a historical research team that's studying American life in the late twentieth century. My group leader thinks I'm at the mall recording shopping patterns." She laughed nervously. "Anyway, as you see, I remembered my promise," the woman replied. "In fact, it came to dominate my entire life. In college, I studied high-energy physics and mathematical chaos theory, all with the hope of discovering the secret of time travel. Finally, when I was twenty-five, I received my doctorate in Applied Mathematics . . . which is when I was contacted by The Project."

"The Project?" Natalie repeated in confusion.

"The time travel project," the woman said quickly. "The U.S. government had been working on it for years. In fact, they're working on it right now. But you won't know about it for another twelve years."

"Then it's going to happen!" Natalie gasped. "I'm going to become a time-traveler! This is fantastic!"

"No, Natalie, it's not," the visitor said, a note of deep sadness creeping into her voice. "The reason we need the time travel project is because the world—the *future* world—is in a really big mess. Global warming—The Greenhouse Effect—turned out to be a lot more serious than anyone ever imagined. Whole areas of the Midwest have turned into deserts. There is worldwide starvation. New diseases are cropping up everywhere. People are dying by the millions. Our mission is to see if there's any way we can change history—*our* history—to stop the devastation before it even begins."

"Well, what can *I* do?" Natalie asked helplessly. "I'm just a kid."

"I know," the visitor nodded. "And I have serious doubts there's anything any of us can do."

"Why do you say that?" Natalie asked fearfully.

"Because, dear Natalie, I remember every word of this conversation from the time a woman appeared at my door during my thirteenth birthday party and told them to *me*," she said. "From that point on, I did everything I could to change the future she told me about, including changing my *own* future. I tried *not* studying physics and *not* joining the time travel project. But various circumstances always conspired to set me back on course. I now know that the future like the past is basically set. The only difference is that I—and now you—know how our lives will turn out."

Suddenly, Megan poked her head outside.

"Hey, Natalie, are you coming to your own party or what?" she asked.

Natalie look helpless from Megan back to her future self. "Uh, go on back to the party," she told Megan, who was now looking at the visitor with wide eyes.

"That's not—" Megan began in awe.

"Go back to the party," Natalie repeated firmly. "I'll be right there."

Obviously shaken, Megan turned and hurried back inside the house.

"You'd better go," the visitor said, taking Natalie's hand in her own. She smiled weakly. "Kris Weller is just about to drop her fruit punch."

Natalie peeked back through the door. She saw her friend Kris Weller holding a glass of fruit punch as she talked to Megan. Everything looked fine. She turned back to the visitor, but the woman was already hurrying down the front walkway. A moment later, she climbed behind the wheel of a rental sedan, fired up the engine, then sped off into the night.

Megan joined Natalie at the front door the minute the shaken birthday girl returned. "That wasn't the future you, was it?" she asked.

"No, of course not," Natalie quickly replied, then forced a nervous laugh. "It was just a friend of my mother's who dropped by to wish me a happy birthday." She smiled as convincingly as she could. "Come on, let's party."

Closing the door, she considered what the visitor had said. Despite the woman's insistence that the future was unchangeable, Natalie still had to believe that people were more than just robots playing out some ancient cosmic program. In fact, she believed that if she could alter even a small part of the scenario her future self had outlined, then maybe she could change the end result as well.

Inspired, she turned toward Kris Weller, who was standing across the room about to refill her punch glass. "Kris!" she shouted. "Don't fill that cup!"

Startled, Kris turned toward Natalie and, in doing so, banged her elbow against Natalie's mom, who had just exited the kitchen carrying another plate of pizza bagels. The next moment, Kris lost her grip and her half-filled punch glass went spinning to the floor.

At that moment, another shiver ran through Natalie's body. But this time, it wasn't the winter wind that chilled her to the bone. It was the knowledge that the future—*her future*—had already begun.

GOOD DEAL

Jeremy Belasco's eyes were as cold as steel. "I'd kill for that comic book."

Mr. Kraken, the neatly attired owner of Kraken's Kollectibles, brushed back his oily gray hair and bent down over the glass-walled display case Jeremy was peering into. "No need to go quite that far," he said, flashing his unnaturally white teeth. "I'm certain we can come to some other equally equitable arrangement."

As Jeremy watched eagerly, Mr. Kraken pulled a small silver key from his vest pocket, opened the back of the case, and removed the plastic-covered comic book as gently as if he were handling a fragile butterfly. Beaming, the man set the book down on the glass counter top just inches from Jeremy's face.

"*Commander Cosmos*," Mr. Kraken announced. "This is Issue 4, in which our hero meets his archenemy, Baron Volton, leader of the Raynkyn Alliance."

Just looking at the thirty-year-old comic book, Jeremy felt his mouth water. He *wanted* it. He wanted it more than he wanted to pass his next history exam. He wanted it more than he wanted to visit the DinoWorld prehistoric theme park. He wanted it *so* much, he *could* see himself doing just about anything to get it.

"How much?" Jeremy asked.

"Two hundred and thirty-five dollars," Mr. Kraken said without missing a beat.

"Ouch!" the boy exclaimed. "That's a lot of money."

"In mint condition, this particular comic has a blue book value of three hundred dollars," the owner noted. "I've lowered the price because there's a tiny stain on the back cover."

Jeremy again returned his attention to the *Commander Cosmos* comic book. He couldn't care less about a little old stain. Cosmos had been one of his heroes ever since he'd started collecting comics at age seven, and he now boasted one of the best collections of *Commander Cosmos* comics in town. Among his most prized possessions was Issue 22, which introduced the commander's girlfriend, "the lovely but humble" Margo Placebo. He also had Issue 67, which featured Margo's tragic death at the hands of Baron Volton's Mold Men. He even had Issue 10, where the intrepid spaceman acquired his now legendary starship, the *Comet's Tail*. Having Issue 4 would make him the envy of every kid in his junior high school.

"I've got fifteen bucks," Jeremy said, reaching for his wallet. "Could I put that down and pay the rest later?"

"You're too young for credit," Mr. Kraken replied.

"How about layaway?" Jeremy proposed.

"Why don't you go for something more affordable?" Mr. Kraken suggested. "Say, an issue of *The Flea.*"

Jeremy considered the older man's suggestion, but deep in his heart he knew he'd never be satisfied with a compromise. As Commander Cosmos himself was fond of saying, "Victory must be absolute!"

"I have a whole bunch of *Amazing Boy* comics," Jeremy offered, referring to a now-defunct action title. "Will you take them in trade?"

"I already have all the *Amazing Boys* I can handle," Mr. Kraken replied, gesturing toward a massive bin.

"What about *Armageddon 3000?*" Jeremy asked.

"No market," Mr. Kraken curtly replied.

"There has to be *something* we can trade," Jeremy insisted. "I mean, I *really* want that comic book. I'll give you anything. Anything at all."

"*Anything?*" Mr. Kraken asked, peering over his wire-rimmed glasses. "Do you really mean *anything?*"

"Well, anything I *have,*" Jeremy emphasized.

"Hmmmm," Mr. Kraken muttered, tapping his stubbled chin. "I'll tell you what, give me a few days to check my inventory. I'll see what I'm short on. If you can help me out, perhaps we can come to an arrangement."

"Excellent," Jeremy exclaimed. Thanks!"

"My pleasure," Mr. Kraken said with a mischievous twinkle in his eyes.

●　●　●

"What's the most valuable thing I have?" Jeremy asked his brother Lewis that night as the two of them sat in his room playing video games.

"That's an excellent question," Lewis replied attentively. Although Lewis was only twelve—two full years younger than Jeremy—he had an IQ of 156 and was therefore considered a genius in many circles. He went to a special school for gifted children and spent much of his time reading books that even college kids found confusing. If anyone was going to help Jeremy figure out how to buy that *Commander Cosmos* comic book, it would be his kid brother.

"Of course, you do have a number of valuable possessions, such as this whole video game system," Lewis noted, at the same time using his hand-held controls to beat the living daylights out of Jeremy's martial arts warrior on the screen in front of them. "But since they're used, you wouldn't get much for them. And of course, you have your comic books—"

"Not for sale," Jeremy interrupted, trying his best to keep his warrior out of his brother's reach.

"Then there are those things that some people say make a person *truly* rich," Lewis continued. "You know, things like friends and family. Why do you ask?"

Jeremy grunted as his warrior was pounded into oblivion by his brother's computerized alter ego, and the game automatically reset itself to play another round.

"I went to Kraken's Kollectibles after school," he explained. "He's got Issue 4 of *Commander Cosmos.*"

"Blue book valued at three hundred dollars," Lewis recited from memory. "In mint condition, of course."

"Kraken is selling it for two-thirty-five," Jeremy said.

"That's a good deal. Take it," Lewis advised.

"I don't *have* two hundred and thirty-five dollars!" Jeremy snapped, made doubly angry because his new virtual warrior was now taking the same awful beating his last one had suffered. "I've got to come up with something else to give him. Something valuable."

"Well, then I guess that really depends on what Mr. Kraken *wants*," Lewis noted. "Value always depends on a combination of supply and demand. For something to be worth anything, people have to want it, yet it has to be rare enough so that not everyone can have it. Do you see what I'm saying?"

"Yeah, I think so," Jeremy replied, not sure he really understood his brother at all. "It's just that the only rare things I have are my *Commander Cosmos* comics. And to sell part of my collection to buy another issue would kind of be defeating the purpose."

"Sounds like you've got yourself a real problem," Lewis said. With that, he hit a series of buttons that blew his big brother's last player off the screen and established himself as the winner.

Jeremy sat there in stunned silence, overwhelmed by both his money problems and the speed with which his kid brother had just beaten him.

●　●　●

Jeremy returned to Kraken's Kollectibles two days later. A bell tinkled, announcing his entrance and attracting the attention of Mr. Kraken, who was busy dusting a shelf of 1960s-era lunch boxes.

"Jeremy!" he said with a smile. "How are you today?"

"Just great," Jeremy replied, his eyes darting over to the case of super-rare comic books. He was relieved to see his prized *Commander Cosmos* still right there. "So, did

you think about what I can give you for Issue 4?"
Jeremy asked hopefully.

Mr. Kraken strolled over to the display case. "She is
a beauty, isn't she?" he remarked, unlocking the back of
the case and gently taking out the comic book. "Except
for that little stain, she looks as fresh and colorful as
she did the day she left the publisher's."

Jeremy gulped nervously. Mr. Kraken was obviously
trying to make him want the comic even more than he
already did. This could mean only one thing—Mr. Kraken
intended to ask him for something *big*.

"Did you figure out what other comics you need?"
Jeremy asked, trying to steer the man back to the subject
at hand. "Is there *anything* I can trade you for it?"

"I gave the matter a great deal of thought," Mr.
Kraken replied. "Understand, I run a very special kind
of business here. I buy rare items—often unique, one-of-
a-kind pieces—then I sell them to people who wish to
own unusual things. Sometimes they want comic books.
Sometimes it's lunch boxes. Other times it's old records,
dolls, or sports cards. Whatever I buy and sell, it's
always an item that brings people pleasure. People will
always pay for pleasure, don't you agree?"

Jeremy's anxiety was growing by the second. All he
wanted from Mr. Kraken was a straight answer—like
"Give me twenty dollars, ten issues of *Rodent Man,* and
a signed 1990 Barry Bonds baseball card." But instead
the man was giving him his whole philosophy of life.
Jeremy didn't know where this conversation was
headed, but he did know he didn't like it.

"So now you ask me, what do I want for this rare
and valuable comic book?" Mr. Kraken went on, gently

stroking the comic's plastic wrapper as if petting an animal. "You don't have the two hundred and thirty-five dollars I requested, so you'll have to give me something else. Something you value at least as much as this item, if not more so."

"You want the rest of my *Commander Cosmos* collection, don't you?" Jeremy snapped. "Fine! You can have it! You can have it all! My comics, my video games, everything! Just stop torturing me like this and give me Issue 4!"

Mr. Kraken just stood there, his face frozen in an expression of absolute shock. At that moment, Jeremy realized that his outburst had not only been uncalled for, it must have sounded like the ravings of a total lunatic. He quickly tried to explain himself.

"I—I mean, over the last two days, I've been wracking my brains to figure out what you'd want," he stammered. "The thing is, I'm just a fourteen-year-old kid. I don't have all that much."

"I understand," Mr. Kraken said sympathetically. "But rest assured, I have no desire to take all your comics and video games."

"That's a relief," Jeremy said with a sigh.

"Material things are, in the end, shallow and meaningless," the man went on matter-of-factly. "In fact, Earth is one of the few places where they have any significant value at all."

"What?" Jeremy asked in confusion. "What do you mean, *Earth?* Where else is there?"

"The universe!" Mr. Kraken declared. "Millions of worlds circling billions of stars in trillions of galaxies. And then there are the *other* universes, other *dimensions!*

There are countless intelligent beings all searching for the same thing—fun—and they're all willing to pay through the nose for it!"

Jeremy couldn't believe what he was hearing. Could it be that Mr. Kraken actually traded collectibles to beings in other *dimensions?*

"You know what collectors *really* want these days?" Mr. Kraken went on, his eyes blazing with delight. "Humans! You wouldn't believe how rare human beings are on other planets! Why, in the Eighth Quadrant of Alternate Universe Seven, humans are fetching up to a hundred zlotniks each! Especially genius humans—like your brother, Lewis. Oh, he'd fetch a premium price this time of year. So what do you say, Jeremy? This comic book for your brother?"

"No way!" Jeremy cried. "You're not getting your grubby hands on my brother! Not for a comic book! Not for *anything!*"

Jeremy was out the door before the bell on the door even had a chance to tinkle. Driven by a sense of terror he'd experienced only in his worst nightmares, he pedaled his bike like a maniac until he came careening up his home driveway. Not even stopping to lower his kickstand, he dropped the bike, raced into his house leaving the front door wide open, bounded up the stairs, and burst into his brother's bedroom.

"You—you'll never guess what just happened!" he said, gasping breathlessly.

"You'll never guess what just happened to *me!*" Lewis interrupted. He reached down and picked a polished wooden box off his bed. "Look at this! It's a chess set that belonged to Albert Einstein! I got it this

morning at Kraken's Kollectibles! Mr. Kraken wanted a thousand dollars for it, but I was able to make a trade. He gave me the chess set—for *you!*"

"*Me?*" Jeremy gasped, his mouth suddenly turning to sandpaper.

Just then, he heard something move behind him. Spinning around, he saw Mr. Kraken standing in the hallway, his oily silver hair glistening in the glow from the overhead skylight, his shiny white teeth glistening as he gave an unnaturally wide grin.

"The door was open, so I let myself in," he said with a chuckle. He then pulled an odd-looking device from his pocket and spoke into its microphone. "The shipment is ready for pick-up."

As Jeremy watched in horror, a doorway seemed to appear out of thin air right behind Mr. Kraken. Two creatures that looked like six-foot-tall grasshoppers in metallic space suits stepped through this inter-dimensional gateway and grabbed Jeremy by the arms.

"Lewis, how could you?" he asked his brother pleadingly. But Lewis just gave an embarrassed shrug.

"Sorry, Jeremy, but I really, *really* wanted this chess set," he replied.

"Let's go, Jeremy, your new owners await," Mr. Kraken said with an icy grin. "You're going to like it in Alternate Universe Seven."

With that, Jeremy was whisked away to a parallel dimension where he was kept in a huge glass jar and played with occasionally until he was traded away for two Rigelian slimebats.

Even in Alternate Universe Seven, kids know a good deal when they see one.

IT'S HOW YOU PLAY THE GAME

Mr. Watanabe, Amber Marchand's science teacher, wagged his finger at her. "Remember, Amber, it's not whether you win or lose," he said, "it's what you learn from the experience."

Amber Marchand rolled her deep blue eyes and tried to suppress a groan. Mr. Watanabe, the man who had been after her all year to "work up to her potential," was now telling her that taking first place in her junior high's upcoming science fair wasn't really important. Of course, as the daughter of a celebrated football coach, Amber knew better. Winning *was* important. And since she really didn't want to be in the science fair in the first place—in fact, she rated science right down there with spinach—bringing home a championship medal seemed the only way to make it worth her while.

"Do you understand what I'm saying, Amber?" Mr. Watanabe asked with concern. "I require all my students to participate in the fair because it's important that they come to appreciate the scientific process. It's a way to learn and practice critical thinking. Hopefully, you will grow from this experience. Now, isn't that more important than any trophy?"

"Okay, if winning a trophy *isn't* important, why are there judges?" Amber countered, then quickly answered her own question. "Because the science fair is a contest. And in any contest, there are winners and there are losers." She picked her school books off her desk, tossed back her hair, and headed for the door. "And I, Mr. Watanabe, am not a loser."

With that, Amber exited into the bustling corridor, leaving her teacher with his mouth open. Checking her watch, she saw that she had just enough time to get to her social studies class, which was located at the opposite end of the building.

But as she zig-zagged her way through the obstacle course of students and teachers, Amber couldn't help but think about what Mr. Watanabe had just told her. The whole thing had started when he had discovered her sneaking a look at the science fair entry forms in his desk drawer. She'd explained that she had merely wanted to "scope out the competition," to see what kind of projects she'd be going up against. And this had caused Mr. Watanabe to launch into his "winning isn't everything" speech, a lecture which, the more Amber thought about it, she disagreed with.

If her father had taught her anything during the past thirteen years, it *was* that winning was everything. If you weren't determined to win at all costs, then you were a sitting duck for anyone who was. "Either play to win, or don't play at all," her dad was fond of saying. "If you don't, you've lost before you even start."

One key to winning was knowing your opponents' strengths and weaknesses. This is why Amber had broken into Mr. Watanabe's files and scanned the other registration forms. She likened it to a sports team studying videotapes of their rivals in action. When you knew how the opposition performed, you could play to their weak spots.

Fortunately, Amber had gotten plenty of useful information from the file before Mr. Watanabe caught her. From what she could see, most of the projects entered in this year's fair were pretty lame. As usual, most of the kids were growing mold, collecting butterflies, testing various materials for their electrical conductivity, or doing any of the other dozen science fair clichés that students resorted to when they lacked imagination. Compared to them, her creation of a nutritionally balanced all-junk-food diet already looked like a sure winner.

In fact, the only real threat Amber could see came from Josh Pendergast, an eighth-grade "brainiac" who claimed to be working on a new computer mouse you controlled just by moving your eyes across a monitor screen. Josh won the fair last year when, as a mere seventh grader, he built a fully operational calculator out of nothing but aluminum gum wrappers. Clearly, Josh Pendergast was the man to beat.

But how? Amber knew she wasn't nearly as smart as Josh. Few people were, even grown-ups. Her all-junk-food diet could prove to be the greatest thing since rice cakes, and still, chances were she'd end up eating Josh's dust.

That meant she'd have to play dirty. She'd have to do something to wreck Josh's project or otherwise get him to pull out of the competition. Whatever she did, it had to be clever enough so that even if her efforts were discovered, they couldn't be traced back to her. Truly, this was going to take as much thinking as the science fair project itself.

Arriving at her social studies class just as the period bell rang, Amber immediately whipped out her note pad and began cataloging ways she might undercut Josh Pendergast's chances of walking off with her first-place medal. She was silently debating the pros and cons of spiking Josh's lunch milk with a liquid laxative when she looked up and noticed that her teacher, Ms. Harcovy, was actually talking about something interesting—the use of magic in various primitive cultures.

"It's been proven that, in most cases, the power of primitive magic comes directly from a society's belief in that power," Ms. Harcovy explained. "For example, if you wanted to give someone bad luck, you would lay a spell on him. First, you would perform a ritual that reinforces your belief in that spell. Then you would make it known to everyone what you have done. The subject of your spell, who would also have to believe in magic, would come to consider himself under your spell and act accordingly.

"Even more important," she went on, "all his friends and neighbors would treat him as if he is, in fact, under your magical influence. They'd shun him and freeze him out of communal activities. Soon, the sense of dread and isolation would become so great that the target could actually become distracted and careless and suffer all kinds of troubles as a result. And this 'success' would only reinforce the society's belief in the magic's power."

Randy Weaver, another student in Amber's class, raised his hand. "But what if the subject of a spell doesn't buy all this magical mumbo jumbo?" he asked. "What if he thinks it's just superstitious garbage?"

"Like I said, it's not so much what the individual believes, but what the society believes," Ms. Harcovy emphasized. "Even if he chooses to reject the idea of magical spells, the simple fact that everyone around him treats him like he is under one will eventually wear him down. That kind of unending pressure is almost impossible to resist, even for the smartest and strongest-willed among us."

Amber set her pencil down and smiled to herself. At last she'd found a way to eliminate Josh Pendergast from the science fair.

* * *

Over the next week, Amber fine-tuned her plan. With only five days remaining till the science fair, it was now time for her to put it into action.

Step one required her getting into Josh's backpack. This proved easy, since he always set it behind his chair when he sat down for lunch in the cafeteria. All Amber had to do was wait until Josh was deep in conversation with his other "nerd-o" friends. Then she nonchalantly carried her tray toward him, pretending to be looking for an empty seat.

"Oops!" she cried as she passed directly behind Josh's seat and "accidentally" knocked her fork off her tray.

"I'm so clumsy!" she added for effect as she bent down to retrieve the fork. At the same time, she deftly unzipped Josh's backpack, stuffed her special "present" inside, then zipped the pack closed. Straightening up, she glanced over at Josh's table and was pleased to see that neither Josh nor any of his friends were even paying attention to her.

"Step one done," she muttered to herself, grinning from ear to ear as she hurried off to sit with her own group of friends.

Following her lunch period, Amber had Mrs. Finch's English class, as did Josh Pendergast. This gave her the perfect opportunity to observe Josh's reaction when he found the little "gift" she'd left for him.

Arriving early to class so there'd be no chance of her missing the show, Amber struggled to hide her mounting anticipation as she watched Josh set down his backpack, unzip the main pocket, and reach inside for his textbook.

"Hey, what's that?" Victor Williams, the boy next to Josh, asked as Josh curiously studied the mystery object wrapped in tissue paper. Having seen Victor's entry form, Amber knew that he had entered the science fair with some crazy study about the effects of various daytime talk shows on flowering plants.

"I don't know," Josh confessed. "Someone must have put it in my backpack when I wasn't looking."

"Maybe it's a gift from a secret admirer," Victor taunted. "Who do you know who likes you?"

Quickly, Amber covered her mouth to stifle a wicked giggle as Josh blushed. He wasn't the type to *ever* get a gift from a "secret admirer." She continued to watch with growing excitement as Josh cautiously peeled back the tissue paper.

"Huh?" he grunted, his eyes nearly popping out of his head.

"What is it?" Victor asked, scrunching up his face. "It looks like . . ."

". . . a weird clay doll," Josh said, completing Victor's thought. "The kind of doll people make so they can cast a magic spell on someone."

Indeed, Amber Marchand had done her homework. After checking out a half-dozen books on primitive art and magic from the town's central library, she had found a picture of the weirdest-looking doll imaginable. A decent enough artist, she had sculpted a likeness of the creepy-looking creature from clay and baked it in her mother's oven. She then added several critical details to the fired clay figure, including a few strands of Josh's own hair which she'd recovered from the comb he carried in his back pocket—and which she'd "borrowed" after she'd conveniently bumped into him in the hall several days before.

Now, just about every student in the class was standing around Josh staring at the odd little figurine and trying to determine its meaning. Josh, being the bright kid he was, figured it out immediately.

"I think someone doesn't like me," he said darkly.

You got that right, Amber thought, then immediately went about putting step two into action.

● ● ●

By the end of the day, the entire junior high was abuzz about the awful little doll Josh Pendergast had found in his backpack. Making sure it became the prime subject of conversation wherever she went, Amber did everything she could to fuel the fear and hysteria already swirling around her rival like his own personal cyclone.

"It's designed to bring bad luck to him and anyone who comes near him," she told a group of kids who were in the hall exchanging rumors about the doll. "I heard about a girl over at Middleton School who got one last year," she later told her friends in gym class. "She ended up dying of a disease so rare there hadn't been a recorded case of it in ten years!"

By the next day word had spread like wildfire that Josh Pendergast was not someone you wanted to be friends with. You didn't even want to get close to him. As a result, the boy suddenly found himself given a wide berth in the hallways, he was surrounded by empty chairs in all his classes, and even his best friends were skittish about eating with him during lunch. Amber was delighted to hear that although Josh was doing everything possible to discredit the whole thing as superstitious nonsense, none of the kids were buying it. Even the teachers now eyed Josh with a degree of suspicion.

The morning of the science fair, Amber arrived at school to hear that Josh Pendergast had been forced to pull out of the competition. When she inquired further, she was told that the boy was so depressed that he'd been unable to even get out of bed.

"Gee, I hope he's okay," Amber said, taking secret delight in her success. She figured that she'd spooked poor Josh so badly that his body had responded with some kind of psychosomatic illness. She was certain that, as soon as he calmed down, his health would be miraculously restored. But by that point, she'd be home polishing her first-place trophy.

That morning, she and the rest of the science fair contestants set up their displays in the gym. None of them came even close to Amber's originality, insight, or attractive display—at least as far as Amber was concerned. As the time for judging approached, she visualized herself walking up to accept the first-place medallion over and over again, using a "power-of-positive-thinking" exercise her dad had taught her.

Everything seemed to be going perfectly until, just as the judging was getting underway, Amber noticed a shoe box sitting under the table that supported her display. Not wanting anything to be amiss, she bent down, picked up the box, lifted its lid, and looked inside.

"It can't be!" Amber gasped as she found herself staring into the face of a clay doll even creepier than the one she had given Josh Pendergast.

"No!" she cried, dropping the box and sending it crashing to the floor. Then she turned and saw a dozen people staring at her. "It won't work with me!" she cried to no one in particular. "I don't believe in magic!"

Now half the people in the gymnasium were staring at Amber, unsure of what to do with this girl who—for no apparent reason—was now completely out of control.

"I know who did this," she declared, her mouth twisted in a hideous snarl. "It was Pendergast. That little twerp thinks he can get even with me. Well, it won't work." She spun around and shouted into empty air. "You hear that, Pendergast! It won't work! I'm a winner! I'm a champion! I'm—"

Just then, a horrible stabbing pain gripped Amber's chest. Her hands turned cold and clammy, and her knees buckled beneath her. Gasping for breath, she stumbled back, lost her balance, and fell awkwardly into her display. Several onlookers screamed as the table instantly collapsed, sending both Amber and her entry crashing to the ground.

●　●　●

As a dozen people rushed over to help Amber, Victor Williams—the boy who had sat next to Josh Pendergast in English class—struggled to suppress a victorious smile. Nearby, a man with a cellular telephone was calling 911 for an ambulance, but Victor paid little attention, choosing instead to put the finishing touches on his science fair entry, which he had titled, "The Effects of Daytime Talk Shows on Flowering Plants." Ten minutes later, as a team of paramedics carried Amber away on a stretcher, Victor—all psyched to win the science fair trophy—finally paused just long enough to make sure that the modeling clay residue was completely off his fingers.

THE HOUSE ON SPARROW LANE

As soon as the family car turned onto Sparrow Lane, Mallory Klump was impressed. The street was spotlessly clean and lined with large, beautiful oak trees. Along each side of the road, stately homes of stone and brick stood like miniature castles, each with its own perfectly landscaped yard.

This neighborhood was a far cry from the suburban townhome complex Mallory and her family had lived in since she was born over thirteen years ago. Although modern and well-maintained, the development had been cramped and institutional, with each home looking identical to the one next door. By contrast, each home here on Sparrow Lane was separated from its neighbor by at least thirty feet, and every house had a look that was uniquely its own.

"Here we are, kids!" Mallory's father announced as he turned into the driveway of 266 Sparrow Lane.

Peering over the seat in front of her, Mallory gasped in awe at the residence looming before them. Although she'd seen the photos her father had taken of the place, they hadn't done it justice. The two-story home looked like a small English manor, complete with large leaded-glass windows on the first floor, intricately carved double entrance doors, and a Tudor-style roof.

"This place is beautiful!" Mallory gasped, imagining herself to be a princess in a horse-drawn coach pulling up to the front of a castle.

"It's great!" exclaimed Reggie, her eleven-year-old brother. Not even bothering to wait for the car to come to a complete stop, he unbuckled his seat belt, pushed open his door, and jumped out to take a closer look.

"I still can't believe we can actually afford it," their mother said, staring up at the gorgeous home.

"How *can* we afford it?" Mallory asked. She knew that although her parents both made decent salaries, they weren't exactly rich.

"It's a foreclosure property," her dad explained. "The old owners abandoned the place a year ago, so the bank took it over, fixed it up, put it on the market, and sold it off at a bargain price."

"Like I always say, Mallory, it pays to shop around," her mother said, giving her daughter a sly wink.

"Well, let's go take a look at our new home," her dad said, killing the engine and climbing out of the car.

On the inside, the Klumps' new home was every bit as impressive as it was from the street. The rooms were large and sunny, the tiles and carpets were all spanking new, and even the doorknobs and faucet handles were top quality.

After taking individual walking tours of the five-bedroom house, the Klumps gathered in the spacious, gourmet kitchen to exchange impressions.

"We're going to need new furniture," Reggie noted immediately. "There's no way our old stuff is going to look good in this palace."

"One thing at a time," Mallory's father said with an understanding smile. "The down payment for this place put a pretty big dent in our bank account."

"I can't believe the old owners just abandoned a house like this," Mallory remarked. "Why would anyone walk away from a home as beautiful as this one?"

"The people at the bank think the owners ran into hard times and just couldn't keep up with the mortgage," her mother explained. "That kind of thing happens more often than you think, especially with expensive homes. Some people just get in over their heads."

"Is that going to happen to us?" Reggie asked, his eyes suddenly filled with fear.

"No, sir," his father assured him, tousling the boy's light brown hair. "Both your mom and I have good solid jobs. We have plenty of money."

"Except for new furniture," Reggie corrected him.

"Except for new furniture," his dad agreed.

That night, as Mallory lay in her bed admiring the lovely plaster moldings that ran around the edges of the ceiling, she silently thanked her parents for finding this wonderful house. She thanked the bank for pricing it so cheaply. And most of all, she thanked the former owners who had abandoned it the previous year.

Smiling to herself, Mallory turned over, pressed her head into her pillow, and prepared to drop off to sleep.

But just then, she heard a low, thunderlike rumble and felt the bed vibrate beneath her. Startled, she bolted upright and strained her ears to identify the source of the strange noise. But the rumbling had stopped, and the house was silent—deathly silent.

Maybe it's the plumbing, she thought. And with that, she lay back down on her pillow and fell quickly asleep.

● ● ●

"So you moved into the Beakmans' place, huh?" said Evalyne Winowski, one of three girls who had joined Mallory for lunch the next week at her new school. Evalyne was a tall, skinny girl with short, red hair and matching horn-rimmed glasses.

"You mean 266 Sparrow Lane?" Mallory asked.

"That's the place," Ashley Tobler replied, tossing back her straight, waist-length auburn hair. "Jan Beakman used to be in our class. Until—" She stopped short.

"Until what?" Mallory asked, leaning forward.

"Well, that's the mystery, isn't it?" Lauren Azell noted, her cold, gray eyes boring into Mallory's. She leaned across the table and spoke in a low, measured voice. "You see, Mallory, last year on Halloween night, Jan Beakman and her family . . . disappeared."

"I know," Mallory replied, still confused by the other girls' anxious expressions. "The bank said they abandoned the house. They couldn't meet the mortgage payments or something."

"Is *that* what they told you?" Evalyne asked. Then she and her friends exchanged knowing glances that made Mallory feel increasingly uncomfortable.

"Isn't that what happened?" Mallory pressed on. "If it's not, I think I have a right to know the truth."

Lauren chuckled darkly. "The only people who know the truth are the Beakmans . . . and the house."

"You see, the Beakmans didn't just run away," Evalyne explained. "Or if they did, they didn't take a thing with them. Their car, their furniture, their clothes . . . everything was left behind."

"It was like they just vanished into thin air," Ashley said dramatically. "No blood. No note. No clues at all."

"And you want to know the really weird thing?" asked Lauren, leaning in even closer. "When the police finally broke in, they found every door locked . . . from the *inside*."

"Including the door to the garage," Evalyne added.

"What did the police say happened?" Mallory asked, suddenly finding it difficult to swallow.

"They don't know," Lauren said, a creepy twinkle in her eye. "Most of the cops—in fact, most of the people in town—don't like to talk about it."

"Maybe you can find out," Ashley suggested. "I mean, if I lived in that creepy old house, I'd sure like to know why people who lived there before me vanished without a trace. Wouldn't you?"

Mallory had to agree that indeed she did.

● ● ●

"Yeah, I covered the Beakman story," said Pam Kane, a reporter who had written several articles about the Beakmans' disappearance, articles Mallory had found while looking through old newspapers in the local library.

Now here she was at the paper's main office, speaking to the reporter face to face.

"What can you tell me about it?" Mallory asked.

"What are you doing?" Pam shot back. "Putting together a Halloween piece for your school paper?"

"No, actually, I live in the Beakman house," Mallory replied matter-of-factly.

"You live at 266 Sparrow Lane?" Pam asked with sudden interest. "Well, I guess you have a right to know then. I suppose you've read my articles on the place?"

"Yes, but what I want to know is if there's anything you didn't print," Mallory said.

"Only some background details," Pam replied. "For instance, the Beakmans built the house less than a year before they disappeared."

"Really?" Mallory reacted with genuine surprise. "I thought it was older than that. It sure looks that way."

"They designed it to fit in with the rest of the neighborhood," Pam explained. "They tore down the house that had been there before and put a whole new one in its place. The original house was apparently in pretty bad shape. You see, it had been abandoned for years—ever since its occupants mysteriously vanished."

Mallory gulped hard and a frigid chill ran up her back. She was beginning to see a pattern here, and it didn't look good for her *or* her family.

● ● ●

For the next week, before going to bed, Mallory ran from door to door and from window to window making sure the house was locked up tight. She knew this precaution hadn't saved the Beakmans from whatever grizzly fate had ultimately befallen them, but doing something still felt better than doing nothing at all.

As for her parents, neither of them put much stock in her concerns. "You're getting caught up in a ghost story," her father said.

"These new friends of yours are just trying to scare you with wild rumors," her mother insisted.

Even her brother Reggie refused to believe that they were in any danger. "People don't just disappear," he told her. "There's always a logical explanation for everything."

Mallory wanted to believe her brother and parents were right. She wanted to believe that some supernatural force wasn't going to whisk them all away in the dead of night. But when Halloween finally arrived, she couldn't help but sense trouble in the air. For October 31st was the day that the Beakman family had disappeared, and Mallory could feel deep in her bones that, like it or not, she would soon discover why.

It was around ten o'clock at night, and the last of the trick-or-treaters had come and gone. Turning off the porch light, Mallory's father closed and bolted the front door as everyone started to prepare for bed.

Mallory was in her bedroom about to take off her shoes when she noticed an odd, unpleasant odor in the air. She tried to ignore it, but it became stronger and more pungent with each passing second.

Concerned, she put her shoes back on and hurried out into the hallway. Reggie was already there, his face twisted into a disgusting grimace as he sniffed the air.

"What is that *smell?*" he groaned.

"It smells like rotting vegetables," Mallory said.

"Did one of you leave the garbage out?" their father asked as he and their mother appeared on the landing at the top of the stairs.

"No way!" Reggie cried.

"Well, something certainly stinks!" their mother insisted. "And there's no way I'm going to bed with the house smelling like *this!*"

Together, the four began a search of the house in an attempt to find the source of the increasingly offensive odor. They started in the kitchen, then inspected the dining room, the living room, and both bathrooms. All the while Mallory was thinking that this was the beginning of the end, a prelude to whatever unspeakable horror was about to strike them.

Ultimately, the Klumps' search took them to the home's unfinished basement. As soon as Reggie opened the basement door, it was obvious they were on the right track, for the smell from below was so strong that it hit them in the face with the force of a knockout punch.

"I think something died down there," Reggie groaned, covering his mouth with his hand.

"Stay up here. I'll go check it out," Mallory's father said as he started down the steps. But after about five minutes, he reappeared at the bottom of the wooden stairs. "I can't find a thing," he called up to his family with a shrug.

"I'll help!" Reggie said excitedly, racing down the stairs. "Maybe we'll find a dead body!"

"Slow down, Reggie! You'll hurt yourself!" his mother cried, hurrying after him.

Mallory, afraid to be left by herself, gathered her courage and headed down to join her family. When she arrived in the cold, unfinished basement with its bare concrete walls and low wood-beam ceiling, she found the others gathered around a large metal drain set in the middle of the concrete floor. She assumed the drain had been installed to help prevent flooding, something a lot of basements in this part of the country were prone to during heavy rainstorms.

"I think the smell is coming from down there," Reggie said, peering into the darkness below the grating.

"I think Reggie's right," his mother agreed.

"Maybe the sewers have backed up," his father speculated. "Although I don't see why. There hasn't been any rain for a week."

Just then, Mallory felt a strange rumbling beneath her feet. It was similar to the tremor that had disturbed her sleep during her first night in the house, only it was stronger and lasted longer than the earlier one.

"What was that?" she asked fearfully.

"It felt like an earthquake," Reggie stated.

"There usually aren't any earthquakes around—" Mallory's mother began, only to be stopped short when another, even stronger tremor shook the house.

"Something's definitely down there," her father said in amazement as he cautiously peered down into the drain. "I think I see something moving."

That same instant, the basement began to shake as if a four-engined freight train were thundering through the center of the house. Losing her footing, Mallory stumbled forward and grabbed the wall for support. A moment later, a piece of the floor right next to her erupted as a huge, wormlike creature, like something out of a fevered nightmare, shot up from below.

Mallory's mom barely had time to scream before the monster—which was as big around as the trunk of an oak tree—grabbed her in its gaping maw, flipped its head back, and swallowed her whole.

As for Mallory, she *did* scream as the monster turned on her father, using its thick, scaly head to knock him to the floor before scooping him up and gobbling him down as though he were nothing more than a piece of popcorn.

Terrified out of his wits, Reggie didn't even try to run as the humongous worm-thing came after him next. Instead, he just stood there frozen to the spot in sheer terror, until it sucked him up into its huge, slavering mouth and gulped him down.

Now only Mallory remained. Her eyes darted to the nearby stairs, and for a brief instant she considered making a bolt for freedom. But she quickly realized that any attempt to escape would be in vain. Surely, the Beakmans had tried to flee a year ago, just as the people who had lived on this site before must have attempted to escape. But their fates had been sealed the moment they decided to build a house here, to sink a basement into soil on which humans were not meant to trespass.

And so, Mallory Klump just stood there in stony silence, her eyes fixed straight ahead as the hideous creature of 266 Sparrow Lane spun toward her, opened its enormous mouth, and . . .

● ● ●

"It's beautiful!" Mrs. Spiegel gasped as she and her husband stood in front of the Tudor-style house at 266 Sparrow Lane. "And such a bargain! I can't believe it!"

"Tell me, what happened to the former owners?" Mr. Spiegel asked the real estate agent standing next to him with hope in her eyes.

"No one knows for sure," the agent replied with a shrug. "They just abandoned the property. Disappeared in the dead of night. I guess they couldn't keep up with the mortgage payments. Got in over their heads. So, what do you say? Do we have a deal or don't we?"

Mr. and Mrs. Spiegel looked at each other for a brief second, then turned back to the agent.

"Deal," they said in unison. "How could we possibly pass up a monster bargain like this?"

SOLO FLIGHT

Ever dream that you're flying like a superhero? That's what riding in a sailplane feels like. It's just you and the wind, soaring through the sky free and easy like some huge, magnificent eagle. It's a sensation most kids can only dream about.

I'm one of the lucky ones. My dad has taken me up in sailplanes since I was old enough to wear a crash helmet. I've probably logged more hours in the air than most kids have logged on their bicycles. If I could, I'd spend my whole life riding the air currents . . . and I almost did.

It was the end of June. The big Fourth of July weekend was coming up, and it was also going to be my twelfth birthday. Mom and Dad had a special present in store for me. They were going to let me take my first solo flight. Although I'd flown our sailplane countless times with Dad in the cockpit, this would be the first time I'd be going up all by myself.

"Are you sure I'm old enough?" I asked anxiously when they told me of their plans.

"It's not a question of age, Jonathan, but experience," my father replied calmly. "Anyone can fly a sailplane if they have the right training. Personally, I'd rather have *you* at the controls than half the adult pilots I know!"

"You'll do fine, Jonathan," my mother assured me. Mom was quite a glider pilot herself. In fact, my parents met while soaring past each other at five thousand feet! "Of course, if you don't want to . . . "

"No, I do!" I quickly cut in. "It's just that this kind of caught me by surprise, that's all."

"I remember the first time I soloed," my dad said, his eyes suddenly taking on that weird, faraway look parents have when they start talking about the past. "I wasn't much older than you. It made me feel stronger and freer than I ever had in my life. It's a feeling you're never going to forget for as long as you live, son."

As it turned out, my dad was absolutely right.

● ● ●

"Ready to go, Jonathan?" my mother called from the base of the stairs.

"In a second!" I yelled back. I was in my bedroom getting myself prepared both physically and mentally for my big day. I'd already spent an entire hour putting together my wardrobe, and now I was standing in front of the full-length mirror on my bedroom door, checking myself out. I was wearing my lucky green shirt, my lucky jeans with the holes in the knees, my lucky leather belt with the silver belt buckle, my lucky red socks I'd worn when I pitched my one and only no-hitter, and, of course, my lucky running shoes with barely any tread left on them. There was only one thing missing.

Going over to my dresser, I opened the small jewelry box set on top of it. Inside, nestled among the various pins, commemorative coins, and other assorted odds and ends I'd collected over the years, was a set of silver pilot's wings. They had belonged to my grandfather—my dad's dad—who died before I was even born. My grandfather had been an Air Force fighter pilot during the Vietnam War. In 1966, at the age of thirty-five, he was shot down and killed by a North Vietnamese anti-aircraft missile. My dad, who was only ten years old at the time, was given these wings at his father's funeral. For some reason, the wings had not been pinned to his dad's uniform when his body was buried. My father never wore these wings himself, but thought I might want to when I became a real pilot. This seemed like the perfect time.

I lifted the small metal wings from the box and carefully pinned them to my left breast pocket. Then I checked myself out again in the mirror. The wings hung straight and true, just like I'm sure my grandfather had always flown. I gave myself a crisp salute, then turned and headed out the door.

"So what are we waiting for?" I shouted as I thundered down the stairs. "Let's fly!"

Our sailplane was hangared at the Sky Harbor Airport, which is about fifteen minutes north of town. It was a small private airfield used mostly by recreational fliers on weekends and holidays. This being the Fourth of July weekend, it was as busy as a toy store during Christmas Eve.

The weather was perfect for gliding. The sky was clear and the air temperature was in the mid-eighties. There was a steady ten mile-per-hour wind blowing in from the west, and the humidity was right around sixty percent. I couldn't have asked for better conditions.

Mom and Dad had already arranged for the plane to be ready for us when we arrived. Climbing out of our car, I saw our glider, the *Sky Dancer,* sitting on the grass tethered to the single-engined tow plane that would lift it into the sky.

For those of you who've never seen a sailplane, they're incredibly beautiful, graceful creations. The *Sky Dancer,* for instance, had a narrow, bullet-shaped cockpit, much like a teardrop. Behind that, her fuselage extended back thirty-five feet, tapering into a thin, almost fragile-looking tail. Her wings spanned nearly forty feet, giving her the lift and stability she needed to stay aloft even without the benefit of a motor. Not designed for combat, transportation, carrying cargo, or any other practical concern, the *Sky Dancer* had one purpose and one purpose only: fun.

"Ready to go, Birthday Boy?" my father asked, giving me a warm pat on the shoulder.

"Let's do it," I said, fitting my helmet, which was painted metallic blue and covered with orange and red stars, over my head.

Five minutes later, I was belted into our sailplane's pilot seat. I gave my father a firm "thumbs-up," and he lowered the bubble-shaped cockpit hatch into place. My heart beating wildly, I watched my parents enter the tow plane parked about thirty feet in front of me. Then my helmet radio crackled into life.

"You reading me, son?" my father asked.

"Loud and clear, Dad," I replied into my helmet's tiny microphone. "Let's get this baby in the air!"

Launching a sailplane is a relatively easy task. The tow plane does ninety percent of the work. As the glider pilot, all I had to do was release my brakes and let Dad and Mom use their rented plane to tow me onto the runway and up into the wild blue yonder. My only challenge was keeping my rudder straight.

A few minutes later, we were at almost 5,000 feet and traveling at about 100 miles per hour—slow for an airplane, but fast for a glider.

"Ready to solo, Birthday Boy?" Mom asked over the radio. "I'll bet you're excited!"

My hands were shaking and my throat suddenly felt dry. I took a deep breath, then answered back. "That's a big ten-four. Ready to release."

Releasing the tow line was my job. Taking a deep breath, I reached forward and pulled the lever that disconnected my aircraft from the nylon umbilical cord connecting me to my parents' plane. I heard a clunk as the hook let go, then was thrown forward in my chair as the sailplane instantly decelerated by about twenty miles per hour. Looking straight ahead, I saw Mom and Dad's plane quickly pull away as it suddenly found itself free of its five-hundred-pound load.

Now I have to tell you there are many differences between riding in a sailplane as opposed to a regular engine-powered aircraft. The first thing you notice right away is the sound. There isn't any. In a commercial jet—the kind most people fly in—there's always the dull roar of the engines in the background and a constant vibration you can feel in every bone in your body. In small, private planes, like the tow plane my mom and dad were in, the engines are so loud they're almost deafening, and the vibrations can be so bad they make your teeth chatter.

But sailplanes aren't like that. When you're in a glider, the silence is unreal. There's no roar of jets. No buzz of internal combustion engines. No vibrations to remind you that the only thing keeping you from tumbling to earth is this big, complicated machine with hundreds of parts, any one of which could fail.

This incredible silence was exactly what I was hearing as the tow plane circled back toward the airport and I was left to fly all on my own. For several moments, I just sat back and enjoyed the absolute nothingness of it all. This, I imagined, is what hawks must feel as they circle the skies in search of prey. It's as if you, the sky, and the entire universe are one and the same.

Sitting up, I turned my control wheel to the right, causing my sailplane to bank slightly in that direction. As it turned and I tilted sideways, I scanned the ground for likely thermals, columns of warm air rising off the earth. It's these natural updrafts that allow glider pilots to keep themselves aloft for long periods of time even in gentle winds. Because darker areas—like parking lots—absorb sunlight and therefore heat the air around them, you always want to look for dark or paved patches of earth when flying a sailplane. Fly over one of these, and you can gain a few hundred feet without even trying.

As I mentioned earlier, this was a very bright, sunny day, so I had no problem finding all the thermals I needed. In fact, even after a full hour of circling the Sky Harbor area, I was still managing to keep the *Sky Dancer* at between 4,000 and 4,500 feet above sea level. Heck, the way things were going, I could probably stay aloft all the way till sundown if I wanted to. After that, the air would cool and I'd naturally find myself drifting back to earth.

However, my parents had no intention of letting me stay in the air that long. In fact, exactly one hour after the towline was released, my helmet radio came to life with the familiar sound of my father's voice.

"All right, Birthday Boy, it's time to bring *Sky Dancer* home," he said.

"Aw, Dad, do I have to?" I protested. I was having so much fun, I really didn't want to quit.

"We're going over to the Jacksons for a Fourth of July barbecue. Don't you remember?" he countered. "We're supposed to be there in an hour."

"Ten-four," I groaned in disappointment.

I adjusted my wing flaps to direct the sailplane earthward and at the same time began looking for bright patches of earth around which I'd find downdrafts to help bring me down.

Keeping a close eye on my altimeter, I suddenly noticed the oddest thing. No matter what I did to lower my altitude, the sailplane refused to descend below 4,000 feet!

"Come on, Jonathan," my father said with some irritation. "I know you like it up there, but you can't stay up there forever."

"I'm trying!" I radioed back. "But I seem to be caught in some kind of big thermal. I can't seem to lose altitude."

"Try to turn yourself out of it," my mother advised. "Look for bright patches of earth."

"That's what I'm doing!" I insisted.

Indeed, for the next fifteen minutes, I used every trick I knew to bring myself down, but nothing worked. In fact, I actually ended up gaining more than 200 feet!

Now I was getting scared. All around me I could see other sailplanes rising and falling with no problem at all. At one point, Dad had a friend of his, who was also flying a glider, get in front of me and try to lead me home. Although *his* plane dropped without a problem, the *Sky Dancer* stayed exactly where she was.

"Dad, I don't know what to do," I radioed, my voice choked with panic. "What if I can't come down ever? What if I'm stuck up here for the rest of my life?"

"That's not going to happen," my father assured me. "There must be something wrong with your controls. If nothing else, we can wait till sunset."

And that's exactly what we had to do. For five full hours I circled around and around the Sky Harbor airport, becoming increasingly panicky with each passing minute. Hungry, thirsty, and desperately needing to go to the bathroom, I watched from my aerial perch as the sun sank with painful slowness below the western horizon, then finally vanished from sight. All the other gliders had long ago returned to the ground. I was now completely and utterly alone.

"The temperature's dropping really fast," my mother radioed. "It's already fallen ten degrees in the last hour. You should be down in no time."

Hearing this, I banked the *Sky Dancer* as tightly as I could and tried my hardest to put the sailplane into a spiraling dive. But, just as before, the craft absolutely refused to drop below 4,000 feet.

I'm going to be up here forever! I thought, terrified out of my mind. *A hundred years from now, I'll finally come down, and all they'll find in the cockpit is an old rotting skeleton!*

An hour later, the sky around me was a sea of stars set against a backdrop of inky blackness. I'd never been in a sailplane at night before—this kind of flying usually wasn't done—and the sense of complete isolation could easily drive a person insane. At least in an airplane you always had the noise of the engines to keep your senses stimulated. But up here in a sailplane, with no noise, no light, and virtually no sense of movement, you could quickly begin to feel totally disconnected from any sense of reality.

In fact, I was certain I was going stark raving mad when, gazing out through the bubble cockpit, I saw two eyes staring back at me. Chilled to the bone, I first told myself that I was either looking at my own reflection in the plexiglass, or that it was some distorted reflection of the full moon. The problem was, there *was* no moon shining this night, and the eyes were part of a face that was definitely not my own.

As I continued to examine the face gazing back at me, I saw that it belonged to a man in his mid-thirties. He had brown hair cut in the style of a military crewcut, and his uniform collar bore the bronze oak leaves of an Air Force major.

It took me a moment or two to realize that I'd seen this face before. In fact, it looked out from several framed photographs back home. It was the face of my very own grandfather.

"What are you doing here?" I asked the ghostly image floating before me. "What do you want from me?"

But rather than respond, the transparent face just continued to hang in the air outside my cockpit. It seemed to be looking through me, just as I was looking through it, and for a brief moment, I wondered which one of us was truly the ghost.

Unable to stare at this frightening visage any longer, I glanced down at my controls and saw that I was still holding level at 4,000 feet. And then, as if waking up from a dream, I realized what was happening. My grandfather's spirit was holding me aloft. Maybe it thought it was helping me, or maybe it wanted me to join it in the vast beyond, there was no way to tell. I only knew that I had to get it to release me or I could indeed be stuck up here for the rest of my life.

"Grandfather, it's your grandson, Jonathan," I said, struggling to remain calm. "You have to let me go. I want to go home. I want to see my mom and dad. They're worried sick about me. I don't want to die up here. Please, Grandfather, release me."

But the image just continued staring at me, and my altimeter refused to budge. What more could I do?

And then I noticed something about the spirit's uniform. There was something odd about it. Something was missing. The pilot's wings!

I immediately looked down at the wings pinned to my shirt. Could these be what my grandfather wanted? Could these be why he was keeping me aloft?

Hands shaking, I carefully removed the wings from my shirt. There was no response from the plane. I set the wings down on the floor. Still no change. Finally, I checked my seat belt to make sure the buckle was secure, then unlatched the cockpit canopy and opened it just a crack.

Instantly, a burst of freezing-cold wind hit me in the face, and the shock almost caused me to lose my grip. But I held fast and with my free hand, scooped the pin off the floor and—sad as I was to lose this one solid reminder of my grandfather's greatness—I tossed the wings out into the night. I saw them glisten in the starlight for a few brief seconds, then they vanished from sight.

I released the cockpit canopy and let it fall back into place. Then I locked it securely and made sure it wasn't about to come loose. Finally, I glanced back at the front of the cockpit bubble . . . and saw that my grandfather's face had vanished!

Excited, I glanced at my altimeter and saw that the needle was starting to drop. 4,000 feet . . . 3,950 feet . . . 3,900 feet . . .

"Sky Harbor control, this is *Sky Dancer!*" I said into my radio. "I'm coming home."

Just then the sky around me lit up with a blinding flash. A ball of fire seemed to be heading right for me . . . then seconds later, it disappeared. Stunned, I wondered if I'd just seen my grandfather's angry ghost.

And then it hit me.

"Fireworks," I said to myself with relief. "It's the Fourth of July fireworks!"

The sky around me continued to explode with joyous celebration as I continued my rapid descent. And then, as I turned on my final approach to the Sky Harbor runway, I saw for the briefest instant, my grandfather's image within the glow of the display's grand finale. His pilot's wings were now pinned proudly to his chest. For the first time, he seemed to be smiling. As I smiled back, the glow from the fireworks faded out, and my grandfather's ghost disappeared forever.

THE
STRAY

Louisa McBride had been warned repeatedly not to take the shortcut home from school. Although walking around the long-abandoned Jerry's Jumbo Mart on Lafayette Avenue could shave an entire block off her trip, the route was considered far too dangerous for a thirteen-year-old girl to travel alone.

"It's not safe," her mother told her on more than one occasion. "It's dirty and probably rat-infested. Who knows what diseases you could pick up there?"

"And there are lots of dark places for people to hide," her father always noted. "Don't even think about walking around that old store."

And Louisa usually *didn't* think about it, even when she stayed late at school and was eager to get home, even when the day was so bright and sunny that dangers, if any, would be easily visible from hundreds of feet away. No, usually Louisa obeyed her parents and walked all the way around the block, even going so far as to travel on the opposite sidewalk. The truth was, the old boarded up building gave her the creeps, and she wanted to stay as far away from it as she could.

Her friend, Judy MacDougal, however, was not so skittish. In fact, Judy was known throughout their junior high as something of a daredevil. Years before, she had been the first girl in their circle of friends to try the high dive at the Downtown Community Center pool. More recently, she'd been the first in line to ride the new quadruple-loop "Devastator" roller coaster at the nearby Sea Cliffs theme park. And to everyone's amazement, for her thirteenth birthday, she actually went skydiving with her father.

In light of Judy's reputation for fearlessness, it came as no surprise to Louisa when one fateful Thursday afternoon Judy suggested they take the shortcut past the old abandoned supermarket. They'd been assigned to work together on a school history project, and were going to Louisa's house to study when a storm moved in.

"Let's cut through the lot," Judy suggested, pointing to the empty parking area alongside Jerry's Jumbo Mart. "Hurry, it's going to pour!"

"But I'm not allowed to walk through there," Louisa reminded her friend. "It's too dangerous."

"Climbing out of bed in the morning is dangerous," Judy countered, already starting to cross the street. "Besides, I really don't think there are any mad killers lurking in the shadows getting cold and wet."

"But if my folks find out, they'll kill me!" Louisa explained, joining Judy on the opposite side of the street against her will.

"So who's going to tell them?" Judy asked. Not waiting for an answer, she headed into the lot. "I mean, come on, Louisa, eventually a girl has to start thinking for herself."

Louisa hesitated only a moment before running after her friend. Part of her felt positively terrified as she imagined all kinds of horrors hiding behind the broken windows and the overflowing dumpsters, waiting to jump out and grab her as she hurried past. But another part of her felt strangely exhilarated as she courageously faced danger head-on.

Racing to catch up to Judy, who was now walking confidently down the service alley that ran along the west side of the store, Louisa shuddered. This was the spookiest part of the trip, as the pathway narrowed quickly to form a long, dark alley with the abandoned supermarket on one side and a high brick wall on the other. The alley was filled with piles of long-forgotten grocery store refuse left there by other kids who'd come this way before them. If a person was going to be attacked, this is where it would happen.

"Come on, what are you waiting for?" Judy cried as she motioned for Louisa to hurry up. Steeling herself, Louisa was just pulling up to Judy's side when a dark form jumped into the path in front of them. Louisa's heart nearly stopped as she saw what appeared to be a huge wolf standing not ten feet away, its yellowish eyes glowing in the dim, shadowy twilight.

Louisa stopped short and clutched Judy's arm. "What are we going to do?" she squeaked in mortal terror.

"Oh, calm down," Judy said, shaking free of Louisa's grasp. "It's just a dumb old dog."

Indeed, as Louisa turned her attention back to the beast, she saw that the "wolf" was in fact just a large, brown mutt. About the size of a small German shepherd, his short-haired coat was dirty from months of neglect, and he had a large scar over his right eye, most likely the result of some territorial dog fight. Although he had no collar or other means of identification, the dog's eyes were bright and warm, and he seemed genuinely happy to see these two human visitors.

"Let's get out of here," Louisa said softly, pulling Judy back the way they'd come. "Don't let him touch you. He's probably covered with germs. He might even have rabies!"

"Oh, stop being such a wuss!" Judy scoffed. Slowly, she walked forward, her right hand extended palm-upward. "Hey, doggy," she said in a soft, babylike voice. "You look like a good dog. Are you happy to see me?"

Louisa was amazed at Judy's courage. Louisa never approached strange dogs, even those who belonged to her own friends. After all, you never knew when one would take a move or gesture the wrong way and go straight for your throat. Yet, here was Judy, not only standing her ground against an unknown stray, but actually trying to make friends with him. It was an act of courage—or stupidity—that would only add to the girl's already legendary reputation.

As Louisa watched in awe, the dog inched cautiously forward, sniffed Judy's hand, then gave it a gentle lick. Judy stroked the dog's head, and he sat down to enjoy the attention.

"It looks like you've made a friend," Louisa said, giving a nervous laugh.

"Animals like me," Judy replied, now scratching the dog behind his ears. "They can tell I'm harmless." Then she motioned Louisa to join her. "You try it. I promise, he won't bite."

Still anxious, Louisa carefully approached the dog and half-heartedly held out her right hand. But as soon as the dog turned his attention to her, Louisa fearfully pulled her hand away.

"Oh, stop it, you big baby!" Judy scolded. "I told you, the dog will not bite you. He's as gentle as a pussycat!"

Once again, Louisa reached her hand toward the dog. This time, the animal actually lowered his head to allow her to stroke him. Louisa laid her palm on top of the dog's large head, then gently petted the back of his neck. The fur was warm, soft, and inviting. In fact, it felt so good, Louisa petted the dog a second, then a third time.

"Ooo, you *are* a good dog," she cooed. To this the dog perked up and licked Louisa's fingertips. Louisa could have stayed there all day, but at that moment, a cold wind whipped through the alley and the rain started to fall in earnest. "We'd better get out of here," she said to Judy urgently. "See you later, boy," she added to the dog, then the two girls moved quickly through the remainder of the alley.

They were almost to Michigan Street, which would take them straight to Louisa's house, when they noticed that the dog was following them. Judy waved her hand at the animal, trying to shoo it away. "Go home!" she ordered. "You can't come with us. Go on. Get out of here!" But the dog refused to retreat, following them at a distance of fifteen to twenty feet all the way home.

The rain was falling steadily when the girls finally arrived at Louisa's house. Opening her front door, Louisa turned back and saw the dog standing on the sidewalk, looking at her with sad, pleading eyes, like it wanted nothing more than to come inside and get out of the dampness. Louisa sympathized with the animal's plight, but knew that her parents would never allow an animal—let alone a stray—into their house.

"Sorry, boy," she said sadly. "But you can't come in. Go home. Go back where you came from."

Just then, Louisa's mother appeared in the foyer. "What are you girls doing?" she asked, seeing the two standing in the open doorway. "Come inside. It's pouring out there." It was then she, too, noticed the dog standing at the edge of their lawn. "What's *that*?" she asked.

"He followed us home," Louisa said quickly, making sure to make no mention of the supermarket. "I think it's a stray."

"Well, just ignore it and it'll go away," her mother advised. "Now come inside and dry yourselves off."

Louisa took one last, painful glance back at the dog before entering the house and closing the door. Deep in her heart, she wished that she could at least allow the animal to come inside and wait out the storm. That was, after all, the humane thing to do. But she knew her mother would be dead set against allowing the beast to set even one paw inside their house, so she made no further mention of it, telling herself that the dog had obviously spent most of his life on the streets, and was probably used to it.

However, when six o'clock arrived and it was time for Judy to leave, Louisa was surprised to see that the stray was now camped out on their front stoop. He was just lying there peacefully, sheltered from the storm by the overhanging roof. Louisa's mother, who was preparing to drive Judy home, was equally surprised to find the uninvited guest, and also a little annoyed.

"I'd better call Animal Control," she said, heading for the kitchen telephone.

"Wait!" Louisa insisted. "Can't we keep him? I've always wanted a dog, and I promise to take care of him."

Louisa's mother considered her daughter's request. "I had no idea you wanted a dog," she finally said. "I suppose we can discuss this with your father when he gets home. Then, if you'd like, we can go to a pet store."

"But I want *this* dog," Louisa cried. "He needs me."

Again, Louisa's mother paused before giving her a reply. She looked down at the mutt, who in turn looked back with his two big, sad, watery eyes.

"Well, all right," she said hesitantly. "If your father says it's okay with him, then it's okay with me."

As if understanding that he had just found a home, the dog suddenly jumped up onto his hind legs and began licking Louisa's face.

"Looks like you've got a friend," Judy said with a chuckle. "So what are you going to call him?"

Louisa thought about this for a moment, then replied, "Jerry."

● ● ●

Over the next month, Louisa and Jerry became the best of buddies. Although Louisa's parents originally insisted the dog be kept in the back yard, the wily animal used his big, sad puppy-dog eyes to get himself invited into the house, and finally into Louisa's bedroom, where he took no time making himself comfortable.

Every morning, Louisa got up fifteen minutes earlier than usual so she'd have enough time to feed and walk Jerry before she had to leave for school. When she came home, she fed and walked the dog again, then studied with him resting at her feet. At night, Jerry slept at the foot of Louisa's bed, which gave the girl a sense of warmth and security she'd never felt before.

And then, about a month after Jerry had moved into the McBride home, he and Louisa were walking through nearby Morningstar Park when the dog suddenly bolted away so fast that he yanked his leash clear out of the girl's hand. Before Louisa knew what was happening, Jerry was racing across the grass at full speed as if he was chasing after some invisible prey.

"Jerry! Come back!" Louisa shouted, running after the dog. "Stop!"

At the edge of the park, the dog finally stopped and glanced back, waiting for Louisa to catch up with him. "Bad dog!" Louisa scolded. "Don't you *ever* do that again!"

She was reaching down for Jerry's leash when the unpredictable dog took off again, this time barking wildly as he raced into the street. Becoming more and more distressed, Louisa chased after the animal, terrified that he'd get hit by a car.

At the next corner, Jerry stopped again and waited for Louisa to catch up. Then, just as before, he took off as soon as she was about to take hold of his leash. It went on like this for block after endless block, the dog apparently making sure he remained free while at the same time making equally certain that Louisa never lost sight of him.

Finally, the chase led them to Lafayette Avenue. Barking tauntingly, Jerry dashed into the abandoned Jerry's Jumbo Mart parking lot, raced toward the side alley, then disappeared into the building through a broken window.

"Jerry!" Louisa cried breathlessly, tears welling in her eyes. "Jerry, please come back! Come on, boy! Come out of there!"

Afraid that she'd lost her pet forever, Louisa slowly made her way toward the opening through which Jerry had entered the building. Stepping carefully to avoid the broken glass that lay strewn all over the pavement, she peered into the dim grayness of the abandoned store's interior, then called the dog again.

She heard a distant bark, and hope rose in her heart. Barely considering her parents' warnings to stay away from this place, she squeezed herself through the narrow opening and continued on in pursuit of her dog.

In the years that had passed since the store went out of business, an inch-thick layer of dust had settled over everything, and leaks in the roof had caused many sections of the old linoleum floor to crack and rot.

"Jerry?" Louisa called hesitantly as she made her way up one of the aisles past rows and rows of empty shelves. "Where are you, boy?"

Suddenly, something flashed by at the end of the aisle, then disappeared from sight. "Jerry?" Louisa called again, starting after the elusive animal.

But as she did, a section of the floor beneath her groaned and abruptly gave way. Louisa screamed and flailed her arms wildly as she suddenly found herself falling through a huge hole in the floor. Then, a moment later—WHAM!—she landed on a hard surface while bits of debris rained down on her.

Looking around, Louisa saw that she had fallen into some kind of basement storage area. Painfully struggling to her feet, she moved through the inky darkness until she found a door at one end of the room . . . but it was locked tight.

"Help!" she shouted up toward the hole she'd fallen through. "Can anyone hear me? I'm trapped down here in the basement!"

She waited for a reply, but heard nothing. Now she was getting *really* scared. Here she was, trapped in a dark, damp basement that was probably filled with rats, spiders, and who-knew-what-else, and there wasn't another human being anywhere around. Even when her parents realized she was missing and started looking for her, they'd never think to look in Jerry's Jumbo Mart. After all, they'd forbidden her countless times from even going near this awful place.

I could die down here of thirst and starvation, Louisa thought frantically. *It could be weeks before anyone even finds my remains!*

Just then, Louisa heard movement behind her, and spinning around in terror, she saw two yellowish eyes glowing within the gloom. But almost in the same moment, she realized they held no danger.

"Jerry!" she sighed with relief. "How did you get down here? Did you come to save me?"

The next moment, two more glowing eyes appeared next to Jerry's. Then another pair appeared to her left,

and another to her right. Her heart pounding in her ears, Louisa realized that she was *surrounded* by wild dogs, all of whom were staring at her like predators preparing for the kill. Only one thought now occupied Louisa's mind: *How many more seconds do I have to live?*

● ● ●

What are you doing with this human? the large female dog asked her offspring in a combination of sounds and movements only other dogs could understand. *What is it doing in our home?*

It followed me home, mother, the mutt known as "Jerry" replied. *It likes me. Can I keep it?*

The mother considered her offspring's request for a moment, then gave a short, high-pitched whine that meant, *We'll ask your father. If it's okay with him, then it's okay with me.*

Jerry happily wagged his tail. At long last, he had a pet that was all his own.

HIDE-AND-SEEK

Mark's father handed him a slip of paper. "Here's the number of the restaurant where we'll be in case of an emergency," he said. "Remember, only call us if it's something really important."

"Everything's going to be fine," Mark assured his father. "I'm twelve years old now. I can baby-sit a nine-year old for two hours. Go and have fun."

"Jake, you're to obey Mark while we're gone," their mother instructed Mark's younger brother. "Remember, he's in charge."

"You mean, I have to do whatever he says?" Jake asked fearfully.

"Everything within reason," his mother replied.

"What if he tells me to jump off the roof?" asked Jake. "Or eat a goldfish? Or give him all my toys?"

"I wouldn't do that," Mark scoffed, although the idea of having Jake clean his room *had* crossed his mind.

"No you wouldn't," Mark's mother warned him.

"Let's go, honey," his father said impatiently, opening the front door. "Mark, be sure to double-lock the door after we leave."

"And don't open it for anyone," his mother added.

"I said, we'll be fine!" Mark insisted, motioning his parents out the door.

His parents hesitated another moment, then finally relented and left the house. As soon as the door was shut, Mark tripped the deadbolt lock.

"Did you double-lock the door?" his father called from the other side.

"It's locked!" Mark shouted back, then turned and headed into the living room.

This was Mark D'Angelo's first time sitting himself and his brother, and he was eager to prove he could handle the responsibility. Many of his friends at school had been sitting themselves for months, and Mark had been feeling frustrated whenever his folks had hired someone else to stay with them—especially when that sitter turned out to be a teenager who was only a few years older than he was. For weeks he had been insisting he could stay home alone, and he wanted desperately to be given that chance. Now, here it was. Tonight, Mark D'Angelo was going to prove to the world that he could be a responsible young adult. The fact that his parents were paying him three dollars an hour to do so only sweetened the deal.

"So, what are we gonna do?" Jake asked eagerly.

"Watch television," Mark replied matter-of-factly as he plopped himself down in front of their big-screen TV. "There's a cool movie on cable I've been wanting to see."

"Can we play a game?" Jake asked.

"No," Mark replied, grabbing the remote control off the coffee table.

"But the movie doesn't start for fifteen minutes," Jake whined, pointing to the program guide. "And I want to play a game. When Betty Stevens sits with us, she always plays games."

"Betty Stevens is a nerd," said Mark, referring to the gawky sixteen-year-old who'd been their primary sitter for the past year. "I mean, if she had a life, she'd be out on dates instead of baby-sitting us."

Jake sat in the chair across from Mark and pouted silently for several seconds. Then he glared up at his big brother wearing a particularly nasty expression.

"If you don't play a game with me, I'll tell Mom you took money from her cookie jar," he threatened.

Mark sat up with a start. For years, their mother had stored loose change and dollar bills in a ceramic cookie jar on their kitchen counter. Lately, Mark had been "borrowing" from the jar to buy trading cards, snacks, and other odd items when his allowance money ran out. He thought no one knew about these activities, least of all Jake. And maybe Jake didn't know. Maybe he was just bluffing. But Mark knew he couldn't afford to take that chance. Although he had every intention of giving the money back—it now added up to about $12.75—he knew that if his mom ever found out what he'd been up to, she'd probably ground him for a month just on principle. He couldn't afford to take that chance.

"Fine!" Mark snapped, throwing the remote onto the couch. "I'll play with you for fifteen minutes. What do you want to play?"

"How about *Dragon's Tooth?*" Jake asked, referring to a board game he'd gotten for his last birthday.

"No way," Mark replied. "It's boring."

"You want to set up my road race track?" Jake asked, his eyes dancing with anticipation.

"Takes too long," Mark stated. "I'll miss the movie."

"Then how about hide-and-seek?" Jake proposed.

Mark considered this. They'd used up every decent hiding place in previous games. That meant that any game they might play now would be over in no time.

"Great," Mark agreed. "Hide-and-seek it is."

"I'll count to thirty and you hide," said Jake, turning away and closing his eyes. "One, two, three . . ."

Immediately, Mark ran for the stairs. He bounded up them two at a time, then turned right into the guest bathroom. Treading as lightly as possible, he stepped into the bathtub and arranged the vinyl shower curtain so it hid his body from view.

As hiding places went, this one was pretty lame, but Mark didn't care. He just wanted to end the game as soon as possible. Then Jake would leave him alone.

"Ready or not, here I come!" Mark heard his brother call from downstairs. Instinctively, he held his breath and tried not to move. Although he had no serious hopes of remaining hidden, the competitive part of his nature refused to let Jake win too easily. He was reminded of those times when he had had to abandon one of his videogames right in the middle of a round because he'd been called down to dinner. Sure, he wasn't going to lose money or anything by just walking away from it, and he could work his way back to where he was at any time, but still there was something almost, well, criminal, about not playing your very best. In fact, the hardest thing for Mark to do was to *try* to lose.

"I know you're up here!" Jake called tauntingly as he stood just outside the bathroom door. "I heard you come up the stairs!"

Yeah, a real Sherlock Holmes, Mark thought snidely. *You ought to open your own detective agency.*

He heard Jake step into the bathroom. A moment later, the curtains were pulled back and his brother's eyes glared at him.

"This hiding place *stinks*!" Jake protested. "This wasn't any fun! You didn't even *try*!"

"Hey, I'm twelve years old!" Mark countered. "There aren't that many hiding places I can squeeze into!"

"I want to do it again," Jake insisted.

"Fine," Mark agreed. "But this time, you hide and I'll seek. Let's see how good you are!"

"We have to start in the living room," Jake said, heading for the hallway. "And I'll bet I can hide so well you'll *never* find me."

"Yeah, right," Mark scoffed. "I'll bet I can find you in less than two minutes."

"How much you want to bet?" Jake challenged.

"A quarter," Mark replied, like he was the last of the big-time gamblers.

"Make it fifty cents," Jake countered.

"It's a bet," Mark said as they reached the base of the stairs. "You've got thirty seconds to hide. Then I've got two minutes to find you. Go!"

Immediately, Mark turned around, shut his eyes, and began counting to himself. He heard his brother thunder up the stairs, then heard the groaning of floorboards overhead as the boy searched frantically for the perfect hiding place. Listening closely for any clues, Mark held his breath. A low rumbling sound would indicate that Jake had opened a sliding closet door. The slap of a wooden door closing was a clue he'd climbed into the linen closet. In fact, having played hide-and-seek with Jake for years, he was by this point able to home in on his brother's location from even the subtlest of noises.

"Twenty-nine, thirty!" Mark declared, spinning on his heels and vaulting up the stairs. "I'm coming to get you, Jake! Better have that fifty cents ready!"

Mark's first stop was the bathroom where he himself had hid just minutes before. Although nothing in the sounds Jake had made indicated that he had returned to this room, Mark figured the kid was just sneaky enough to make it *sound* like he'd gone into one of the bedrooms, then quietly double-back and hide in the one place he thought Mark wouldn't bother to look. So, of course, Mark *did* bother to look there, but he found the bathtub empty. "Come out, come out, wherever you are!" he called, checking under the vanity, only to find the usual cleaning supplies and spare rolls of toilet paper.

He next examined the linen closet situated directly outside the guest bathroom, but Jake wasn't in there, either. That left only the three bedrooms.

Deciding to do this systematically, Mark started with his own bedroom. He looked in his closet, under his bed, beneath his desk, and even in his laundry hamper. His brother was nowhere to be found—yet.

A few steps down the hall to the right was Jake's bedroom. Walking gingerly across the minefield created by all the toys that Jake had left strewn about, Mark quickly did a thorough search of the room. Once again, he came up empty.

By process of elimination, this left only his parents' bedroom and bathroom.

"I know where you are, Jake!" Mark announced gleefully. "And I've still got a full minute left!"

Moving quickly, he pushed back the mirrored door to his father's closet and searched it from top to bottom. He checked behind his father's business suits and felt around in the darkness behind his pants. No Jake.

He then did the same inspection of his mother's closet. When he and Jake were younger, both boys had had some success hiding stretched out on her packed-to-the-gills closet, effectively camouflaged by their mother's dresses. This time, Mark wasn't going to be fooled. He plowed through his mother's clothes like a heat-seeking missile. Still no Jake.

With his allotted two minutes about to run out, Mark quickly looked under his parent's bed, behind the bedroom drapes, and then in their bathroom's shower stall. Flustered, he realized his time was up.

"Very good, Jake!" he called into empty air. "You won our bet, but I'm still going to find you!"

Deciding to retrace his steps, Mark again searched each bedroom and bathroom top to bottom. He looked behind bookshelves and potted plants, even though there was no way a boy as big as Jake could have hidden behind them. But Mark was getting desperate.

About to give up and ask Jake to reveal himself, Mark suddenly flashed on the answer: *Maybe, while I was in one of the bedrooms, Jake sneaked back downstairs and is hiding there!* It was the only answer that made sense. Jake had faked him out, making him waste his time *up*stairs when he was really *down*stairs.

"It's over now!" Mark cried as he thundered down the carpeted staircase. "I can smell you down here!"

Moving with increasing desperation, Mark did a top-to-bottom search of the living room, the dining room, the kitchen, and the downstairs bathroom. As each inspection failed to produce any sign of his brother, Mark's anxiety rose a notch. Something in his gut told him that something was very, very wrong. There was simply no way Jake could have hidden himself *this* well.

"All right, Jake, I give up!" Mark finally cried in defeat. "Where are you?" He waited for Jake's response, but all he heard was a deathly silence. "This isn't funny anymore, Jake!" he called, a frightened squeak in his voice. "Now come out and show yourself or I'm not going to pay off the bet!"

Mark looked at his watch. It was already eight o'clock. His movie was starting, and now he was going to miss the beginning because of his stupid brother.

"I'm going to watch the movie!" he shouted. "If you want to watch it with me, you'd better come out!"

He listened closely for signs of movement, but still heard nothing. Now Mark was really starting to worry. He imagined his brother squeezing himself into some impossibly tight space and, unable to breathe, dying of suffocation. Boy, would his parents be upset about that!

"Jake, where are you?" Mark cried, running to the front door in the off-chance Jake had decided to hide outside. But the deadbolt lock was still in place, which meant no one had come or gone since his parents left.

His heart pounding wildly, Mark bounded back up the stairs. Stopping on the landing, he cupped his hands around his mouth like a megaphone and shouted, "Jake!"

"Mark!" came a response. It was Jake's voice, but it sounded faint and strangely far away.

"Jake!" Mark shouted with relief. "Where are you?"

"Mark!" the distant voice called again. "Help me!"

Turning his head from side to side, Mark hurried down the hall toward his parents' bedroom, figuring the calls were coming from there.

"Jake, where are you hiding?" Mark demanded. He paused in the bedroom doorway for his brother's reply.

"I'm over here!" came the faint response. Oddly, Jake's voice now seemed to be coming from the other side of the house, back toward his own bedroom.

"Jake, I mean it! Stop fooling around!" Mark scolded, now feeling an uncomfortable combination of fear and anger. "Just tell me where you are, and I'll help you!"

"I'm back here!" he heard his brother cry. "It's dark!"

Now back in his own bedroom, Mark searched frantically. The faintness of Jake's voice indicated that he was either on the far side of the house, or trapped behind something—like a wall!

Terrified by the possibility that Jake had somehow managed to get himself trapped within the home's superstructure, Mark raced over to his bedroom wall and shouted, "Jake, are you back there? Talk to me!"

He pressed his ear to the papered wall, hoping to hear some sound of movement.

"It's dark, Mark! Help me!" came his brother's tearful plea. But it wasn't coming from behind the wall. It seemed to be coming . . . out of thin air!

Immediately, Mark grabbed a chair, ran over to the air vent above his door, climbed up, and shouted, "Jake, are you in the air ducts?"

"No, Mark, I'm back here!" came a reply so distant Mark could barely hear it.

For the next half hour, Mark raced up and down the stairs calling for his brother. But no matter which room he ran to, Jake's cries seemed to come from someplace else. Finally, Jake's voice grew so faint that Mark was unable to hear it at all. For reasons unknown, Jake D'Angelo had completely disappeared.

● ● ●

Mark's parents returned from dinner an hour later and he told them the whole story in agonizing detail. At first, his mother and father believed the boys were playing some kind of prank—after all, nine-year-old kids don't just vanish into thin air—but the horrified look in their eldest son's eyes finally convinced them Jake's disappearance was all too real. Together, the three of them again searched the house from top to bottom, but not only did they fail to find any signs of the missing boy, they didn't even hear his strange, distant cries for help. Jake was truly gone.

"Where could he have gone?" asked Mark as he joined his mother back downstairs after nearly an hour of fruitless searching. "He sounded so far away. Like he'd fallen into another universe or something."

"I'm going to call the police," his mother declared, moving to the phone. "In the meantime, go back and help your father keep looking."

Exhausted both physically and mentally, Mark dragged himself back up to the second floor. He paused on the landing and looked around for his father.

"Dad?" he called. "Mom wants us to keep looking while she calls the police."

Strangely, there was no reply.

"Dad . . . ?" Mark called again, his voice choking back in fear.

"Mark! Where are you?" he heard his father call. "I can't find you!"

The voice sounded impossibly far away.

"Mom! It's Dad!" Mark screamed at the top of his lungs. "Something's happened to him!"

Seconds later, his mother came bounding up the stairs. "Where's your father?" she demanded.

"I—I don't know," Mark stammered in terror. "I think it's the same thing that happened to Jake."

Confused, Mark followed his mother as she ran into the master bedroom. "George, where are you?" she screamed, her voice gripped with fear.

"Over here!" came the faint reply. "I can't see you!"

Mark watched his mother spin around, trying to find the source of the voice. As she did, she stumbled backward toward the bed—and vanished from sight!

"Mom!" Mark screamed, as he began to reach out toward the spot where his mother had been just a moment before. "Where are—"

"Mark! Stay away from the vortex!" his mother called back faintly. "It's somewhere around the bed!"

"*Vortex?*" Mark called back. "What's that?"

But his mother's answer was too faint to hear.

Shaking, Mark ran to a dictionary and looked up the

word. From what he gathered, *vortex* meant something like the center of a whirlpool. That only meant one thing—his family had been sucked into another dimension!

In that instant, Mark's whole future suddenly flashed before him. He saw himself phoning the police to report the inexplicable disappearance of his father, mother, and brother. His saw a room-to-room search failing to produce any signs of the missing people. He imagined himself being shipped off to a foster home—or worse, to a mental hospital where faceless doctors in white lab coats would work on him day and night to learn the "truth" of what had really happened here this night.

In that same instant, Mark realized he really had no choice. He belonged with his family, wherever they were. And so, his face devoid of emotion, he closed his eyes and fell toward the bed. As he did, only one thought filled his mind: *Wherever I'm going, I hope it's a nice place.*

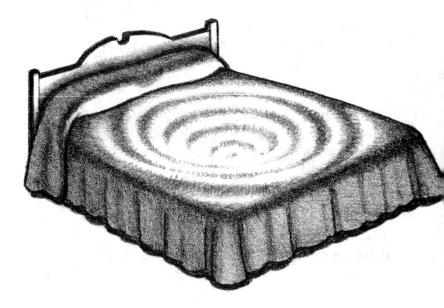